Mango
In the City

A Mango
Delight STORY

BY FRACASWELL HYMAN

STERLING CHILDREN'S BOOKS
New York

STERLING CHILDREN'S BOOKS
New York

An Imprint of Sterling Publishing Co., Inc.

ISBN 978-1-4549-4405-8

Library of Congress Cataloging-in-Publication Data
Names: Hyman, Fracaswell, author.
Title: Summer in the city : a Mango Delight story / by Fracaswell Hyman.
Description: New York : Sterling Publishing Co., Inc., [2020] | Audience:
 Ages 8-12. | Summary: Mango is invited to star in Yo, Romeo! in New York
 City, but must struggle to balance the opportunity of a lifetime with
 homesickness, insecurity, and staying close to her best friend
 long-distance.
Identifiers: LCCN 2019055923 | ISBN 9781454933946 (hardcover) |
ISBN 9781454933960 (epub)
Subjects: CYAC: Theater—Fiction. | Musicals—Fiction. |
 Homesickness—Fiction. | Aunts—Fiction. | African Americans—Fiction. |
 New York (N.Y.)—Fiction.
Classification: LCC PZ7.H9848 Sum 2020 | DDC [Fic]—dc23
LC record available at https://lccn.loc.gov/2019055923

Distributed in Canada by Sterling Publishing Co., Inc.
c/o Canadian Manda Group, 664 Annette Street
Toronto, Ontario M6S 2C8, Canada
Distributed in the United Kingdom by GMC Distribution Services
Castle Place, 166 High Street, Lewes, East Sussex BN7 1XU, England
Distributed in Australia by NewSouth Books
University of New South Wales, Sydney, NSW 2052, Australia

For information about custom editions, special sales, and premium
and corporate purchases, please contact Sterling Special Sales
at 800-805-5489 or specialsales@sterlingpublishing.com.

Manufactured in Canada

Lot #:
2 4 6 8 10 9 7 5 3 1
11/21

sterlingpublishing.com

To Jamaya,
who inspires me to write books
about girls who look like you.—Papa

CHAPTER ONE

School's Out for the Summer!

BZZZZZZZZ! BZZZZZZZZZ! BZZZZZZZZZ!

The buzzing in my head woke me with a start. What was going on? Were there bees in my room? On my bed? On my head? I sat up, swatting the air around me, and then I realized it was my phone that was buzzing! I must've fallen asleep with it right on my pillow—again. I grabbed the phone. It was Izzy face2facing me.

"Hey, girl, hey! Good morn-ting!" she announced.

"Hey. What time is it?"

"Time to wake up!"

"You know, Izzy, one of the best things about summer break is NOT having to get up until you just naturally wake up."

"So wake up naturally then. It's almost eleven. We got things to do, chica!"

Almost every day since summer break started, Izzy and I would meet up and do something. She got me into paddleball, and we were a pretty good team. There was a court in the park close to her house, so we'd spend the afternoon playing or just hanging by the courts to practice flirting with the cute guys playing basketball across the way.

There was this one guy, Hector Osario, who really got Izzy excited. She thought this brown-eyed, bronze-skinned, shaved-head, six-footer was perfection, but he already had a girlfriend, Marcelle, whose mother owned a beauty parlor and had trained Marcelle to do mani-pedis. Marcelle had fingernails so long they curled at the ends! We couldn't imagine how she managed it, but she was known to be the best teen manicurist in town, and one of the toughest girls in the city. I told Izzy to quit batting her eyes at Hector, since he was taken, but she couldn't help herself. Whenever he was on the basketball court across from where we were playing, her eyes followed Hector instead of the paddleball, and we'd lose every game.

"Izzy, Mom, and I were up really late last night."

"Doing what? Wait, don't tell me, bingeing a TV show. Right?"

"Yeah, *Horror High School*. It was so good. You need to watch it!"

"Girl, you know me, I can't watch anything scary. I'd never get to sleep."

"Well, we watched all nine episodes and then I still wasn't sleepy, so I started reading *Beyonce and Bey-ond*."

"The new biography? OMGZ! Can I borrow it when you're done?"

"It's on my phone. Maybe that's why my phone was on my pillow . . ."

"Cool. You have an hour, then meet me at my house. And bring my number one fan. I'm making my super special tres leches just for him."

On the days that Mom and Dada both worked, I was in charge of Jasper. It was not a duty, it was a pleasure for me, because I just loved that little chubby-bubby so much. Yes, sometimes toddlers got cranky and cried, and it was impossible to figure out how to calm them down, but I didn't mind with Jasper because most of the time he was just a happy clown who could always make me laugh.

I wasn't the only one who admired Jasper. Izzy was in love with him too, mainly because my little teddy bear brother had a huge crush on her! Whenever he saw Izzy, he would toddle up to her, hold his arms high to be picked up, and then plant a kiss on her cheek, wrap his arms around her neck, and lay his head on her shoulder. This thrilled Izzy to no end. She declared Jasper her number one fan and favorite boyfriend—at least until Hector Osario saw the light and realized they were destined to be together forever.

Izzy had even autographed one of her 8x10s, framed it, and given it to Jasper. We thought it was so funny, until one night when Mom took it out of his room and he screamed bloody murder! The photo became a sort of security blanket for Jasper. He'd carry it from room to room, wherever he went in the house. Mom thought he was becoming obsessed with the photo and kept trying to wean him off it by offering more appropriate treasures like a teddy bear, a blanket, or a framed photo of his mother, but nothing worked. Dada thought it was funny and no big deal. He'd say, "Margie, leave the boy be. Just because she's his crush doesn't mean Mommy won't always be number one."

Izzy loved the idea of being idolized, even if it was by a toddler. She started sending me selfies several times a day, urging me to show them to Jasper. I never did. I was afraid he'd become obsessed with one of her selfies and never let me take my phone away from him.

"Okay, Izzy, I'll bring him over, but it's gonna take more than an hour for me to wake up, wash up, eat, and get Jasper ready to go."

"Fine. See you in an hour and fifteen! Bye!" She clicked off, and I dropped back onto my pillow. I wanted to get a little more snoozing in . . . but my bladder was urging me to get up. I stumbled out of bed and headed for the bathroom.

After showering, I pulled on a pair of shorts and a T-shirt and brushed my hair into the usual grapefruit-size Afro puff on top of my head. In the kitchen, Dada was feeding Jasper his homemade baby food: mashed up yam, cinnamon, and coconut milk. It made the kitchen smell great—and it was really yummy. Whenever I fed Jasper, I'd help myself to some, too—a spoon for him and a spoon for me.

Dada smiled and looked at me with pseudo-astonishment and said, "Mango gal, since when ya legs get so tall and ya hair reach the sky so?" I stuck out my tongue at him, then laughed and poured a bowl of cereal.

"Any big plans today?"

"I'm taking Jasper over to Izzy's. She's making him a special treat. Then we'll probably go to the park."

"Sounds like the perfect summer day. I'm gonna change my little homie here, and then I have to get downtown and meet a couple about catering their anniversary party." He lifted Jasper out of the high chair and headed out of the kitchen.

"Good luck with that."

"Who needs luck when you've got mad skills?" I heard him laughing all the way down the hall.

———

Anywho, the day my perfect summer took a sharp left turn off Right Street, I was pushing Jasper in his stroller out of our apartment building. Who should be standing out front next to the skinny tree dogs used as a pit stop? Bob! My teacher from Trueheart Middle School. It took me a moment to recognize him, because . . . well, number one, he was not in school where he belonged. Whenever I run into someone who is not in the place where I usually see them, it takes me a few moments before I remember who they are. I bet I wouldn't even recognize my mother at first if I walked into my classroom and saw her there. The second reason I didn't recognize Bob is because he was wearing shorts and a T-shirt. Now Bob, who insisted all of his students use his first name, wasn't the type of teacher to wear a shirt and tie, but cutoff jeans and a New York Knicks T-shirt? This was *totally* out of character, even if he was the most fun teacher I've ever had.

I was pushing Jasper's stroller out the front door, when I heard . . .

"Mango! Heeeeyyyyyy!"

I turned, and someone started walking toward me. Immediately I took a step back, because like I said, for a few moments there I'd been about to shout out, "STRANGER DANGER!" But then I saw jazz hands and open arms and a shock of red hair that stood up like a cockatoo, and I realized it was just my favorite teacher in the last place I would expect to run into him.

"Bob? What are you doing here? Do you know someone in my building?"

"Yeah. You."

"You came to see me?"

"Right again."

"Well . . . why didn't you ring the bell and come up?"

He wiped the beads of sweat streaming down his forehead with the back of his arm. "I had your address on the contact list from the play but not your apartment number. I tried to call, but the phone was disconnected."

"Oh, yeah. Since my mom, dad, and I all have cell phones now, we decided to cancel the landline."

"Right. I get it. So, I thought I'd just come stand out here and wait until you came out."

"Suppose I didn't come out?"

"Then I guess I'd get a worse sunburn than the one I'm working on right now."

He did look a little hot pink on the verge of scaly-flaky-itchy red, and I felt sorry for him, so I said, "Wanna come up?"

"Are your parents at home?"

"No, they're both working."

"Well . . . I think it would be more appropriate for us to hang out here. What are you up to today?"

"I'm on my way to Izzy's. She's Jasper's favorite star and she made a special tres leches dessert just for him, so he can fall more madly in love with her."

"Huh? Uh . . . never mind. Can I walk with you? There's something I'd like to talk to you about."

I shrugged. "Okay, but maybe we should find some shade in the park and sit down. You look like a showerhead someone forgot to turn off."

He put his hand over his heart pretending to be offended. "Heeeeyyyy, big guys drip in the heat, what can I tell you?"

I laughed and he tickled Jasper under his chin, and then we started walking. When we got to the park, Bob bought three cones of shaved ice from the Icy Man, and we sat on a bench under the shade of a big, leafy tree. The Icy Man had given me extra napkins because Jasper was drooling red juice all down his chin and onto his clothes, but it was so hot out, I didn't care and let him enjoy himself.

Bob held the paper cup of shaved ice to his wrist. "This cools your temperature down. Did you know that?"

"No."

"Well, now you do. Learn something new every day, and you'll always be smarter than you were the day before."

Bob wiggled his eyebrows as he laid his line of wisdom on me, and I was reminded of how funny he was in class and how much fun it was being directed by him in the school play. He was the best director ever. I truly believed that, even though he was the only director I'd ever worked with. He had taken a girl—me—who had never done any acting or singing in front of anyone before and made me a star . . . at least in my school. Because of how Bob encouraged me, boosted my ego, and even kicked my butt a little when I needed it, I was actually dreaming of having a career in show business as a singer and actress.

Bob asked me how I was doing and how the summer was treating me and blah, blah, blah, until I raised my hand and said, "Aren't you the one who told us all good writers cut through the small talk and get to the meat of a scene as quickly as possible?"

"Why yes, I do believe that sounds like something genius I would say."

"Well . . . cut to the meat!"

He laughed and slurped a big chunk of his green ice, before starting again. "First of all, I want to let you know that Larry and I—Mr. Ramsey to you—we're not coming back to teach at Trueheart next year."

Whoa! Cutting to the meat is one thing, but dropping a bomb like this? This truly did call for a setup, some idle chitchat, laying some groundwork before dropping the big KA-BOOM! If he and Mr. Ramsey, the music teacher he collaborated with on our school musicals, were not coming back to school, would we even get to do a play at all the next year? I'd been so looking forward to doing another show and getting back together with all my dramanerd friends.

I had to admit it, I was hooked on theater, and this was the worst news EVER. Yeah, maybe Principal Lipschultz would hire another teacher who would want to direct the school play, but it wouldn't be the same. No one was as much fun as Bob. What if it was a teacher who insisted we call them by their last name, and it was something like Knucklebacher or Bumplehurst or some other weird name that would make everything so formal and yuck? Even worse, what if he or she didn't think I was talented and I didn't get a part in the show?

"No, Bob, noooo! You can't leave Trueheart! We love you and Mr. Ramsey. We need you!"

"Heeeyyyy, we love all of you too, but we have an opportunity that's impossible to pass up. That's what I wanted to talk to you about."

At that moment, Jasper dropped his shaved ice on the ground and began to wail. I gave him mine, and he quieted down the minute he stuck his tongue on it. I couldn't eat anyway. This news was the most devastating ever.

Bob put a hand on my shoulder. "Listen to me. Larry and I have found a backer who wants to put up the money for us to do a summer showcase of *Yo, Romeo!* in New York. Off-Broadway. Actually, off-off-off-off-wayyyyyy-off Broadway."

I gasped. "That's like, uber-crisp, right?"

"So crisp it's downright crunchy! We'll get all kinds of people to come see the show, especially people who invest in theater. If they like the show enough, they could move it to Broadway. I mean, the *real* Broadway. And then Larry and I would be on our way to fulfilling our dream."

"That's great. Really great, but are you sure you want to leave Trueheart?"

"We're sure. We can't do both. If the show gets picked up, we'll have to be available. Larry and his wife, Stephanie, have already packed up and moved to Harlem. That's in New York City. His family has a brownstone there, and I've been camping out in their basement. Once she gets a leave of absence from her job, my girlfriend is going to join me and we'll rent our own place."

"You have a girlfriend?" I shouldn't have sounded as surprised as I did, but, well, to be honest, I wasn't sure Bob liked girls . . . you know?

"Yes, I have a girlfriend. Her name is Raven. We have a daughter together, Josslyn. She's four. She'll be coming up to New York, too."

"Wow!" My head was spinning from all this new information. Also because it was amazing that I was having a conversation like this with a teacher! It was like we were just, you know, friends and he was sharing his life with me. Bob had always been the coolest of all my teachers, but we'd never talked like this. It helped me focus less on what I was losing and more on how this would be life-changing for Bob and Mr. Ramsey. I couldn't expect them to put their dreams on hold because a bunch of middle school kids and I would be lost without them. I produced my biggest smile and held my arms open wide for a hug. "Come here, you!"

He held his hands out in front of him. "Sweaty! Excessively sweaty!"

Ew. So I just took his hands and squeezed them as tightly as I could. "I really am happy for you. And it was so cool of you to come and tell me. Who else knows?"

"No one."

"Oh." That was a surprise. "Why tell me before anyone else?"

"Mango, you don't get it, do you?"

11

"Get what?"

"The reason I was standing in front of your apartment building like Frosty the Snowman in July?"

I screwed up my face and shrugged. Whatever he was pitching, I wasn't catching.

"We want you."

"Me? For what?"

"To come to New York and star in the show, of course! Who could possibly be a better Juliet than you? You're perfect!"

And that's when Jasper decided to throw his arm up, launching what was left of his shaved ice and red syrup into the air. It all came down on my head like a cherry ice shower, but I didn't care, I was too busy imagining myself going to New York to star in a show!

CHAPTER TWO

Stars in My Eyes

A couple of hours later, Bob, Mom, Dada, and I were seated around our kitchen table. The adults were having a serious conversation, and I was just sitting there like a kid, arms folded across my stomach, which was aching in anticipation of a decision.

The hands of the kitchen clock were creeping past 7. Mom was still wearing her red Target manager shirt, which she usually changed out of the minute she got home. Dada got up from the table to check on the oxtail stew that was simmering in the dutchie on the stove. Jasper was seated on the floor by the fridge, stacking and knocking down blocks again and again. Oh, for the carefree life of a toddler instead of being on pins and needles while grown-ups discuss your fate, your future, and what's best for you without turning even once to ask you what you want.

"You mean to tell me, Mr. Bob"—even though Bob had asked, Mom refused to be casual with a teacher and call him just by his first name—"that you couldn't find any

13

other actress in all of New York City to play this part?" "Exactly. After a week of auditions, we did see some who looked perfect for the role, but they couldn't sing as well as Mango. And the few who had really good singing voices were either too old or just not right for Juliet. We even tried to work out a deal with Destiny Manaconda."

Suddenly, the ache in my stomach was completely forgotten. Destiny Manaconda was the star of *Cupcakers,* my favorite television show. Actually, it was Brooklyn's favorite show and mine, back when we were besties. Before she accused me of drowning her new cell phone on purpose, we'd call each other and watch it together every week. Since the show ended, Destiny Manaconda became a huge pop star *and* the girlfriend of my BCF (Boy Crush Forever), Gabriel Faust. He's so cute, so uber-crisp, that I have a life-size poster of him hanging on the inside of my closet door. I leapt up from my seat. "Destiny Manaconda! She's going to be in *Yo, Romeo!*?"

Bob shook his head, "Well, no. She wanted to get paid . . . a great deal of money, and since she has a hit song on the hot one hundred, her people are sending her out on a radio festival tour."

"That's right, she's going to be in the WXRX Summer Jam with—"

Mom's hand jutted out like a traffic cop. "Hello! Can we get back to the topic at hand here?"

I sank back down, and Bob cleared his throat and continued, "Sorry, uh, Destiny didn't work out, and I think it's for the best. She a great singer and all, but she lacks a certain quality that Mango brings to Juliet. Seriously."

A certain quality? I wondered what he meant. I mean, I was just plain old me.

Bob was doing his best to sell Mom on the idea. "Believe me, Mrs. Fuller, Larry and I tried our best, but we couldn't find anyone more perfect than your daughter."

Mom shook her head no and she pulled off the band that held her locs back in a ponytail, "I'm really sorry, Mr. Bob. I mean, I loved your show and you're right, Mango was terrific in it, but . . ." She ran her hand through her hair. "She's only twelve—"

"—Which is why she is perfect for Juliet!"

Uh-oh. Bob had just interrupted Mom. No one EVER interrupted Marjorie Nadine Fuller and lived to tell.

Mom held up her traffic cop hand to quiet him. "She may be perfect for whatever, but she's too young to be traipsing off to New York City all by herself. Her father and I are working people. We can't just take the summer off. It's just impossible. Who would take care of her? See to it that she's safe and fed and following the rules?"

"I've already thought of that!"

Mom twisted her lips and dropped her chin to her chest. "Oh, you have, have you?"

"Yes. You see, my sister, Ziporah—we call her Zippy for short—she lives in Brooklyn, just a short subway ride from where we'll be rehearsing. She's in the show too, so we figured

Mango could stay with her. Zippy would be her chaperone."

"An actress?" Mom laughed. It was not a nice or funny laugh. No. It was a dismissive, *you must be out of your mind* kind of laugh, and I could see the color of Bob's sunburned pink skin deepen to purple.

"Do you really think we're going to let our little girl go to New York and shack up with some someone we don't even know or trust? Come on now, Mr. Bob. I don't mean to be rude, but what kind of parents would we be if we'd give in to such foolishness?" She went on laughing as she looked over at Dada, seeming to expect him to laugh along with her, but he looked like he was deep in thought.

Bob was quiet and slumped forward a bit. I took a deep breath as I watched my dreams of an exciting summer in the Big Apple fizzle away. Yes, I wanted to say something, but arguing with Mom was like trying to win a battle with a tank when all you were armed with were spitballs and a straw. Then an idea popped into my head and I couldn't help myself. I blurted out, "What about Aunt Zendaya?"

Dada, who was standing at the stove putting the lid back on the pot, chimed in. "Yes, that's a great idea!" To me, his voice sounded like a bugle announcing the arrival of the cavalry coming to save the day.

Mom's laughter wound down abruptly, she slowly turned to me, "What about her?"

"She's my aunt. She's family."

Mom shot back, "I've known my butter-brained sister a

lot longer than you."

Her tone was sharp, and for a minute it felt like all the air had been sucked out of the room. Dada put down the wooden spoon he'd been using to stir the pot, lowered the heat on the stove, and came to the table to sit across from Mom.

"You and I both know we can trust Zendaya with our children. She's their auntie, and she loves them. She'd be over the moon to have Mango for the summer. She's been bugging us about it for years. And we both know we can trust Mango to take good care of herself. We trust her to take care of Jasper by herself when needed."

"I know, but—"

This time, Dada held his hand up, though more like an orchestra conductor than a traffic cop, shushing Mom. "Hear me out, okay? It would only be for, what, six weeks?" He looked to Bob, whose shoulders were beginning to reinflate.

"Yes, only six weeks. Four weeks of rehearsal and a two-week run of the show."

"She'd back home in time for school?"

Bob's whole body began to reinflate with hope. "Oh yes, definitely. No matter what."

Dada leaned across the table toward Mom. "Think of the experience she'd have. Instead of sitting around the house here all summer, watching TV and hanging out, Mango could learn what it's like to have a real job by going to New York and doing a show with professional actors. It's an amazing opportunity!"

"Are you serious, Sid? You can't be. I don't believe you could want this."

"*She* wants it." Everyone turned to look at me. "Look at that sparkle in her eyes. She's been a changed girl since the first night of *Yo, Romeo!*" Dada said to Bob. "You should see the way she floats around here, singing the songs from your show over and over. I've even caught her looking in the mirror acting out her role when she thought no one was watching."

"Dada!"

"It's true, I've seen you. So tell me, Mango, do you want to go to New York and do the play?"

"More than anything. Yes!"

Dada turned to Mom. "We can keep her here and she will be frustrated and resentful all summer, or we can let her go and allow her to grow and learn and blossom."

Mom seemed to consider it, then shook her head no.

I spoke up, "Destiny Manaconda was ten when she started out, and look at her now."

Dada joined in, "What about that boy whose poster you have inside your closet? What's his name again?"

I'm not sure why, but at the mention of my BCF, I felt the heat rise in my cheeks as I answered, "Gabriel Faust?"

"Yeah, that's the one, wasn't he like five years old when he starred in the TV show you couldn't get enough of? You liked him too, Margie! You'd always crack up laughing when he'd say in that squeaky little voice, 'Brats rule, fools drool!' Remember?"

Mom didn't say anything. Instead she got up and walked across the room to pick up Jasper. She grimaced when she got a whiff of his diaper and left the room to change him.

Dada watched her leave and then turned to Bob. "When will you need Mango in New York?"

"Uh . . . Monday would be great. I know it's just a few days away, so if that's too soon, we could rehearse a couple of days without her, seeing as she knows the part and all."

"We'll do our best to get her there for the first day. We'll have to work things out with her aunt."

"Of course." Bob stood and held out his hand, and Dad rose to shake it. "Thank you so much," Bob said, "Really, thank you!"

"No. Thank you for giving my girl this opportunity."

Bob nodded and turned toward the door. "I'll have our producer call you with all the details."

Dada said, "Where ya think you a goin', suh?" His Jamaican accent was bursting from his mouth like a breeze from the island, blowing all the tension away.

"Uh . . . I was . . . leaving?"

"Come now, mon, no one step in Jamaican kitchen with di food dere cookin' and leave with dem belly not be full. Sit down and eat!"

I had never loved my Dada more than I did at this moment. My eyes overflowed with grateful tears. I blurted, "I'll start packing," and ran to my room before I started blubbering and embarrassing myself in front of Bob.

I was wiping my eyes on my T-shirt when I saw my phone on the bed. There was a text message from Izzy.

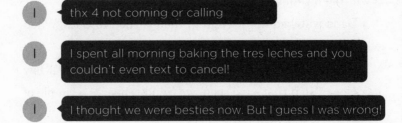

thx 4 not coming or calling

I spent all morning baking the tres leches and you couldn't even text to cancel!

I thought we were besties now. But I guess I was wrong!

Oh no. I had been on my way to Izzy's so Jasper could enjoy the dessert she'd made just for him when I ran into Bob, and . . . in all the excitement, I completely forgot about Izzy. Talk about butter-brained! I had a lot of apologizing and explaining to do.

CHAPTER THREE

Memories to the Rescue

M y thumbs tap danced across the keyboard:

I fell back on my bed and waited for a response. And waited. And waited. Nothing came. Ugh! The sun was finally going down, so it was too late to run over to Izzy's and apologize, on my knees, in person. I'd do it in the morning. First thing. I wouldn't lie in bed until afternoon. I'd get up early, dig out Dada's recipe for blueberry scones, make a batch, and take them over to Izzy. The aroma would force her to open the door (Dada had made them for breakfast the morning after we had a sleepover, and she'd been begging for more ever since).

"Hey."

I looked up. Mom was at the door. I waved and she smiled, which was a surprise, seeing how she had left the kitchen in a silent fury. It was rare to see Dada go against Mom, especially in front of someone else. They never shared their disagreements in front of me. Never. I'd lie awake at night hearing them "hash things out" when they thought I was asleep, but I'd never seen it happen with my own eyes.

Mom stepped into the room. "So, which do you want to take? The duffle or the suitcase?"

"The suitcase," I said, surprised by her change of heart.

"You'll probably need both, since you'll be gone for six weeks." She walked across the room and sat on my swivel desk chair. I could tell her prosthetic leg was bothering her. Mom had lost a leg in a car accident back when she lived in New York and was going to Brooklyn College. Working as a manager at Target and being on her feet eight hours a day was hard on her, but she never complained. She didn't want us to worry or for Dada to feel guilty that he lost his job as a chef. Yes, Delicious Delight catering was doing better than expected, but the only way we would have affordable health insurance was for Mom to go back to work full time. My mom was a champion and I know she wanted me to be one too.

"You really want to go, huh?"

I wanted to beam but tried to hold my smile in check, because I didn't want to make her feel like I was gloating. "Yes, I really do."

"I'm gonna miss you."

"I'll miss you, too."

"No, you won't."

"Yes, I will. I promise."

"Mango, honey, I don't want you to miss me. I want you to be so busy with your work and taking in New York and new experiences that you won't have time to miss nothing but the subway train." She laughed. "Actually, after a few days, you'll probably despise the subway. Going from Brooklyn to Manhattan and back every day can be a frustrating mess. The noise. The filth. The rats the size of bulldogs."

"Bulldogs!"

"I'm exaggerating a little bit. Trying to trick you into changing your mind."

"I won't, Mom."

"I know you won't, and I don't want you to. Not really."

I sat up all the way and leaned toward her with my elbows on my knees. "How come you changed your mind? I mean, a little while ago you were against it."

"I was. I am. But your father brought back a memory that broke through my hard head."

"What memory?"

"When I was about your age . . . no, I was actually sixteen. It was the year before me and Dora lost our parents."

"Zendaya, Mom."

"Yeah. Right. That was before she changed her name, too.

But I ain't gonna get into all that." She sighed and swiveled the chair from side to side for a moment, "Anywho, as you say, the coach at my high school helped get me a scholarship to spend the summer training in track and field at SUNY Purchase. It was a college, not more than a couple of hours from Brooklyn. I mean, it was still in New York. The same state. But my mama absolutely refused to let me go."

"No!"

"Yep. I begged and pleaded with her and my dad. It was all right with him, but Mama would not be moved. Mr. Guastefeste, my coach, came over and tried to talk some sense into Mama. He explained how much an experience like this could benefit a girl like me, with so much potential. But Mama shook her head and said we couldn't afford it. Coach told her it was free. A scholarship. Everything was paid for." Mom swirled the chair toward the window and straightened her prosthetic leg out in front of her. "Mama asked him if the scholarship was going to pay for the babysitter they'd have to hire to look after Dora all summer. You see, that was my job. From the time she could hang a key around my neck and teach me to lock and unlock the door, Mama put me in charge of my little sister. That was my full-time summer job. No pay involved."

Mom didn't say anything for a while. I wanted to ask her to go on, but her eyes were far away. All of a sudden, she snorted and shook her head. "My mama, one hand on her hip, stood up and led the coach to the door saying, 'Her potential can do just as good running around the high school track

24

where I can look out my window and holler to bring her back home.' Then she opened the door and darn near pushed Mr. Guastefeste out."

"Whoa."

"Yeah, Mama didn't play."

"Guess that's where you got it from, huh?"

Mom turned toward me, eyebrows raised and said, with a posh accent, "Why, whatever do you mean, my dear?"

I fell back on my bed and laughed. Mom came and lay down next to me, looking up at the ceiling. She groaned a little and rubbed her leg.

"Your leg is hurting you, isn't it?"

"No, it ain't so bad. Nothing a little ibuprofen won't see to."

I turned toward her and raised up on my elbow. "You know, if me going away is going to make it super hard on you, I'd rather stay."

"I know you would, baby. But the hardest thing on me would be knowing that I snatched your chance to follow your dream right out from under your nose the way my mama did to me."

"Were you mad at her?"

"I was. Oh my goodness, I hated her all that summer. I wished all kinds of bad on her that I regret to this day. Really. I carry the guilt from the things I . . . things I never said out loud." She covered her mouth with her hands and shook her head as though she were shaking the memories away. She turned away as she wiped at her eyes. I looked the other way to give her a moment of privacy and because . . . well, it's kind of scary to see someone as strong as my mom cry.

"You know," Mom said, "as you grow older, you begin to see things in a different light. I understand now that what my Mama was doing, she was doing out of love. She felt she was protecting me by keeping me close. It was hard for her to trust anyone, and I know now that she believed she was keeping me safe. That's what she believed." Mom turned back toward me, her eyes glistening, "I guess I was feeling that way too, until I realized that my need to keep you safe was wrong if it meant keeping you from growing and following your dream."

A thought popped into my head, and I sat up on the bed. "What about Jasper? Who's going to take care of him if I go away?"

"Don't worry, Mango. Mrs. Kennedy will take care of him when your father and I are at work."

"But you'll have to pay her."

"This adventure of yours is worth it, and besides, with you gone, we'll have one less mouth to feed."

I wrapped my arms around Mom and buried my head into her armpit. She smelled like a mixture of deodorant, cocoa butter, the coconut oil she used to moisturize her locs, and the sidewalk after it rained. I curled into her real tightly, wanting to inhale her protection and her love, to imprint them in my mind, so that I could have them close, no matter how far I was from home.

Dada yelled from the kitchen, "Anybody hungry back there? Come get it, or this hungry white boy and me are gonna chomp it up like a couple of harbor sharks!"

Mom and I chuckled, and we squeezed each other tighter for a moment, before relaxing. Mom sat up first. "You know, I'll be on you like green on peas if I hear anything about you misbehaving or breaking my rules, you hear me?"

"Yes." I smiled.

"And you know your Aunt Zendaya thinks she's some kind of Zulu warrior rebel woman, and I don't want none of her habits rubbing off on you. You are going to call me every night at bedtime, ten o'clock."

"Ten? In the summertime?"

"You're going up there to work, so you can't be staying up all hours. You hear me?"

"Yes, Mom."

"Now that you've got a phone, I can keep close tabs on you, and believe me, that's just what I'm gonna do. You understand?"

"Yes, I understand you, I hear you, and I love you." I wrapped my arms around her again, breathing in her scent, happy and grateful to know how deeply she cared.

—

Dinner was hilarious. Bob kept us laughing with stories about the New York auditions and how wonderful most of the performers were, but the few weirdos that came through were the ones he'd never forget. "There was a young woman who came in to sing for us. She looked like she'd make a fine Juliet, but when she started singing, she did a headstand. Larry and I were completely baffled! After she finished her song, she explained that it was easier for her to stay on pitch while upside down. She thought it would be a cool idea, to play Juliet with a new perspective on her world." Bob wound up with a stomachache, because of how fast he was talking and eating at the same time. He hardly chewed his food, he was inhaling it so fast.

Dada got Aunt Zendaya on speakerphone, and she enthusiastically agreed to let me spend my summer vacation with her. She was so ecstatic, she started gabbing on about all the things we would do and all the places she had to show me. "Girl, I'mma take you over to Flatbush where me and your mama grew up. We'll go shopping at King's Plaza Mall. Remember how we used to haunt that place, Marj? Walk around for hours not buying a thing, just pretending to shop 'cause we ain't had two nickels to rub together. Oh! And then we have to spend some time up in Harlem and down by Washington Square Park and NYU in the Village, my old stomping grounds—"

"Pump ya brakes," Mom called out, "Dor—uh . . . Zendaya, Mango is coming up there to work. I'm gonna put her on a strict schedule and expect you to hold her to it."

"Yes, ma'am, sister-mama. Aye-aye, sir! Roger that! I aim to please, captain!"

Dada, Bob, and I laughed. Mom gave us a tight smile and laid out the rules she expected me to follow. "Hold on," Zendaya said. "You don't expect me to memorize all of this?"

Mom joked, "I don't expect you to remember your name as many times as you've changed it."

"Don't start with me, Marj."

"Remember that time you changed it to Eczema, until you found out it was a skin disease?"

Everyone burst out laughing, even Aunt Zendaya. She said, "Do you really want to take this stroll down memory lane over the phone? 'Cause I got plenty stones to kick in your path if you do."

"Never mind all that. I'll send you an email with all my instructions tomorrow. You still have an email address, don't you?"

"Actually, texting me works better. Email is so ten years ago."

Mom rolled her eyes, "Texting it is, as long as you get it."

The mention of texting reminded me of Izzy—and how I totally stood her up today. I said goodbye to Aunt Zendaya and Bob, and as I started clearing off the table, I went over my plan. First thing in the morning: make blueberry scones, take them to Izzy's house, and fall on my knees and beg, kiss her feet, lick the soles of her sneakers, whatever I had to do to win her forgiveness. I knew I wouldn't have a good time in New York unless I made things right with her.

CHAPTER FOUR

Me and My BIG MOUTH!

Okay, so I didn't wake up as early as I had planned. It was hard to fall asleep with visions of New York City dancing in my head! Mom and Dada had taken me there to visit a few times, but that was all before I was five so I didn't remember much. Most of the things I knew about New York came from movies. I knew next to nothing about Brooklyn, the place where Mom and Aunt Zendaya grew up.

Whenever someone was rude to Mom or if someone cut her off in traffic, she'd have to hold herself back from cursing, saying, "Please, don't make my Brooklyn come out—not today!"

That was what she called her aggressive side, and what Dada called her fire breath. I once saw the full force of her Brooklyn side when Mom and Aunt Zendaya got into a huge argument—Aunt Z had borrowed money from Dada but then forgot or neglected to pay back. This was the year Mom was pregnant with Jasper and, well, let's just say I wished on a star that night that the baby would be a boy, because sisters could really go at it when they fought.

Eventually, they forgave each other. They always did. They were family, more than sisters, because after their parents died in a horrific fire when Mom was seventeen and Aunt Z was ten, Mom practically raised Aunt Z on her own. Mom didn't like to talk about it, but Aunt Z loved telling stories about the way they grew up. When I got to New York, I wanted to find out as much about that time—and Mom—as I could.

I crawled out of bed at around 11:30, unplugged my phone, and gave texting Izzy another shot.

I waited. And waited. Finally, I got up and went to the bathroom. How was I going to get Izzy to respond? She couldn't stay mad at me forever. We were this close to being besties. I was being careful about whom I gave that title to, especially after what had happened with Brooklyn.

I had truly believed Brooklyn and I would be best friends forever. We were alike in so many ways. Neither one of us had phones, we both had the same favorite TV show, *Cupcakers*, we both liked to run and joined Girls On Track together, and my dad was the chef in her dad's restaurant. It was like fate had brought us together. But then Brooklyn got a phone, and the rest was misery. We just couldn't be friends anymore, especially after I accidentally drowned her phone in the girl's bathroom sink and she wouldn't or couldn't forgive me. Then she tried to set me up for humiliation by putting my name on the list to audition for the school musical. But I showed her—I sang anyway and got the lead role in the play. Her plan backfired, and she wound up transferring to another school. And I promised myself that I would be very careful about choosing my next bestie.

Izzy was cool, and we had so much in common now that we both were wild about theater and being actors and singers and stuff. Also, Izzy was teaching me how to flirt with boys. She was good at it, and even though I was N-O-T ready to have a boyfriend, I wanted to learn so I could be ready for when I *was* ready.

When I checked my phone, there was still no response from Izzy. I decided to text a juicy headline. Something she couldn't resist.

M bob was here last night. guess u don't want to hear scoop about bway

It took less than one second for the dots under my text to start pulsing, letting me know Izzy was texting me back.

lunch? I

M where?

MCDs I

M when?

When I emerged from my room, Dada was in the kitchen sharpening his cooking knives on the big stone block he had brought with him from Jamaica. He had taught me how to do it when I was little, so I knew my way around knives and how to slice meat and veggies like a professional chef. Seriously, my knife skills were *on point fa true*! I usually liked to help Dada when he was doing stuff like this, but I had to get ready to see Izzy, so I said a quick good morning and hustled toward the bathroom for a shower.

"Breakfast, Sleeping Beauty?"

"No thanks."

"I made crème brûlée French toast."

That stopped me in my tracks. Why did anything with the word "French" in the name always taste so good? French fries, French dressing, French bread, French dip, and best of all, French toast. But Dada only made crème brûlée French toast when there was something to celebrate, so I said, "What's the occasion?"

"Your mom. She was such a good sport about you going to New York, I wanted to celebrate her before she left for work."

"But she's on a diet."

"Not this morning, she wasn't." He laughed.

I looked at the golden brown wedges of French bread and my mouth watered, but I resisted. "No thanks."

"You sick?"

"No, I'm meeting Izzy for lunch and she hates going out to eat with people who don't eat."

"Fine. Turn down a chef when he's sharpening his knives."

I went over, got on my tiptoes to give him a kiss on his bristled cheek, and asked, "Can I borrow five bucks? Pretty please, with crème brûlée on top?"

—

Izzy was placing her tray on a table when I rushed into McDonald's. I had run all the way, because I didn't want to be late. I was held up because of the French toast I couldn't resist sampling—if you could call three pieces drizzled with maple syrup sampling. I jogged over to the table. "I made it!"

Izzy checked the time on her phone. "In the nick of time. Now get some food and spill the tea!"

I ordered a chicken wrap off the dollar menu, hoping I could at least force it down. When I got back to the table, Izzy hadn't touched her food yet. She really hated to eat alone. As soon as I sat down, she bit into her Quarter Pounder and signaled for me to begin.

"Well, first of all, I'm sorry about yesterday, but so much happened that—"

"You forgot me. I know. You're forgiven. Press fast forward and skip to the good part."

"Fine. So, I saw Bob and he told me that he and Mr. Ramsey are not coming back to Trueheart next year."

I shouldn't have said this when she was sucking soda through her straw, because she almost gagged and some of her Dr. Pepper spewed out of her nose. It was gross. I ran for more napkins. When I got back to the table, Izzy was coughing, so I wiped up the mess.

"OMGZ, what, are you trying to kill me?"

"You said fast forward."

"I know, but dang! You cracked my face and broke my heart all at once."

"That's not even the half of it," I said.

"There's more?"

"Lots."

She held a finger out toward my lips. "Okay, hold on. Let me take a sip before you go on." She took a long drink, sighed, and said, "Proceed."

Izzy's eyes grew wider and wider as I told her all about the New York showcase of *Yo, Romeo!* and how it might go to Broadway if it was a hit.

"Shut up, up and away! Are you serious?"

"Yes! And here's the best part. I'm going to New York to be in the show!"

Her eyes sparkled with excitement. "That's amazing! They're taking you?"

"Uh-huh."

"What about me?"

"You?"

"Yes, of course me. Don't they want me to be in the show, too?"

I paused. "Oh. I don't know."

The sparkle in her eyes flickered a bit. "You didn't ask?"

"No, I was too shocked that they had asked me."

"So, you didn't think about your friend? Just yourself. Wow. No wonder you stood me up."

"Hey, you said you forgave me!"

"For standing me up, yes, but for forgetting about me, that's a whole other crime."

"It's not a crime, Isabelle. Just a . . . I don't know . . ." I trailed off, trying to figure out what to say. "I guess I just assumed he was going to ask all of us to go."

"You did?"

"Yeah! I mean, you were a big hit in the show. We all were, so . . ." My mind swooped back to the stories Bob had been telling last night about auditions. He hadn't really said anything about having cast the other parts yet, but . . . something told me I had just put my foot in my mouth and not mentioning the New York casting sessions tasted like a big fat lie.

"You're right! OMGZ!" Izzy stood up and threw her arms in the air. "We're going to be on Broadway!"

All heads in the McD's turned toward her. She started pretending paparazzi and fans were stalking her. "No autographs, please! I love you! I love all my little Izzy-addicts! Okay, just one more pose! Make sure I get a copy of those pics, Joe!"

"Joe? Who is Joe?"

Izzy sat back down and pulled out her phone. "He's a photographer from *Variety* I made up. I've been visualizing him following me throughout my whole career, taking pictures of me everywhere I go. For the publicity."

"What are you doing?"

"I'm sending a group text to the gang, to let them know we're all going to Broadway!"

All of a sudden, the crème brûlée French toast was trying to force its way up from my belly and onto my tray. I clamped my jaw and took a deep inhale, trying to calm my stomach.

"Hold on, Izzy. I don't know if we're all going for sure."

"We better be. Why start all over when he already has a great cast? That doesn't make any sense. Besides, remember how he kept telling us if we did our best we might make it to Broadway?"

"I don't remember him saying that exactly."

"Not in those words, but that's what he meant." Izzy's phone started vibrating, and she glanced at it. "OMGZ, Braces Chloe is in Vermont at the camp she hates. She's going to beg her mother to get her a ticket home right away."

I imagined myself grabbing Izzy's phone and dunking it into her supersize Dr. Pepper, but I had been super careful about touching anyone's phone since I'd drowned Brooklyn's old one. So no, I didn't snatch her phone, but I should have stopped Izzy and cleared things up right that second. I should have told her the truth about the auditions.

Then I started thinking that Bob *should* take Izzy to be in the New York show. She was great as Juliet's agent! She got more laughs than anyone else. I decided to call Bob and talk him into it. Then Izzy could come with me and she wouldn't be so mad when I told her the truth—I was pretty sure none of the rest of the cast was going to New York.

As soon as Izzy headed home, floating on cloud nine thousand ninety-nine, I called the number Bob had saved to my phone last night. As soon as he answered, I immediately launched into how great Izzy was in the play and how it wouldn't be the same without her and how she should come to New York with me. I held my breath waiting for him to speak, hoping he would agree with me.

It seemed like forever, but finally he said, "Izzy is great. I mean, she's wonderful." Bob paused. For a second, I thought we had been disconnected, but then he cleared his throat. "I have no doubt she's going to be a big star. Humongous!"

"Then you'll invite her to New York to be in the show, too?" I pleaded.

"Mango, you don't understand . . ." His phone beeped. "Uh-oh, my battery is dying. Listen, I have to explain quickly. This is not a middle school production anymore. Nobody is going to believe a twelve-year-old girl is a singing star's agent."

"Well, how come they'll believe a twelve-year-old girl can be Juliet?"

"Because, Juliet and Romeo really are about twelve or thirteen years old. And we've already cast my sister, Zippy, as the agent and—"

I heard a loud beep as his phone died—along with my master plan.

CHAPTER FIVE

The French Lesson

My phone blooped and blooped for hours, alerting me to text messages. They were from Izzy, but I was too much of a coward to answer her texts. Then texts started coming in from other kids who had been in *Yo, Romeo!* All of them wanted to know when we were leaving for New York. Izzy even called! I didn't pick that up either. I was a cramped muscle, and I didn't know what to say or do. I needed time to gather the courage to break the news—and Izzy's heart. And now, I also had to break the hearts of the entire rest of the cast because I hadn't had the guts to stop Izzy from spreading news that wasn't true earlier.

I literally could not sleep, so I was awake at four in the morning when my phone got a face2face alert. I glanced at the screen—it was Hailey Joanne calling from Paris, where she and her mother were doing a monthlong French immersion course. I accepted the call.

"Bonjour! Comment vas tu?"

"Huh?"

"Mango? It's me, Hailey Joanne. Why is it so dark there?"

"Uh . . . because it's four in the morning here."

"Oops! It's ten in the morning here in Paris. I wanted to chat with you over breakfast. I'm so sorry. Between the French lessons and couture fittings and Mother comparing me to all the petites and perfect French girls, I can't keep the six-hour time difference in my head!"

"It's okay, I wasn't sleeping anyway."

I reached over and turned on the lamp next to my bed. When I went back to the screen, Hailey Joanne gasped. "Sacré bleu! Someone has been having un très mauvais summer!"

"Huh? English please."

"You look horrible!"

I looked at myself on the little video square on my phone, and she was right. I had forgotten to put on my sleeping bonnet, my hair was sticking up like the bride of Frankenstein, and I had dark circles under my eyes and crusty drool down the side of my mouth. That was weird, because I only drooled when I was asleep and if I wasn't getting any sleep, how come I was drooling? Oh no! Don't tell me I was becoming an awake drooler on top of all my other problems!

Hailey Joanne took a bite out of what she claimed to be the world's best and flakiest chocolate croissant and said, "Honestly, I called to have a gripe session about maman, but it looks like you're the one with the bigger problems, so . . . flush les toilettes, as they say. I'm listening."

I didn't quite know what she meant by flushing the toilet,

but I just dove in and spilled all the tea about the play, going to New York, and how I'd ruined everything by not setting things straight with Izzy from jump.

Hailey Joanne shook her head, giving me the saddest eyes that ever crossed the Atlantic. "Ooh la la, mon petit chou! C'est dommage!"

I sighed. "Either speak English or add subtitles to your phone, Marie Antoinette."

Hailey Joanne dabbed a linen napkin at the corners of her mouth. "What I'm trying to say is, you've mucked up your life once again. Something great happened. You've been cast in a play and you're going to New York, but because you have this phobia about being direct and letting someone get mad at you, you've made a disaster out of what should have been a triumph!"

I grimaced. "Wow. That was like a punch in the gut."

"Good. You deserve it. Now get off the phone with me, call Isabelle, drop the malware, and leave it to her to get over it. You've got a lot of planning and packing to do. And guess what?"

"What?"

"Good news to go along with the bitter pill you have to swallow."

She grinned at me, took another bite of her croissant and chewed uber slowly. I was about to burst waiting. I needed good news right now! "What good news?" I shouted, "Hurry up and tell me before I digitize, travel through the Internet to Paris, find you, and make you choke on that chocolate croissant!"

Hailey Joanne giggled. "Okay, okay. I was dragging it out on purpose because the news is that good. Mother and I are coming to New York in a few weeks, and I should be able to see you in the play."

"Shut up!"

"Shut me up!"

"OMGZ, that's great! Why are you coming to New York?"

"To see you, of course. That and mother and I have fittings for the wedding."

"Wedding? Whose wedding? Not yours?"

"Of course not mine. You stole the only guy I would ever marry, remember?"

"I never did no such thing!"

"I'm just kidding!"

A part of me wasn't sure how much of what she said was kidding. You know, every joke had a little, teeny-weeny, itsy-bitsy grain of truth in it. And TJ, the boy she had been crushing on in school, did like me instead of her. But it wasn't something I had planned. It had just turned out that way. And anywho, TJ and I weren't boyfriend and girlfriend, just friend-friends. At least, I was trying very hard to convince myself that we were only friend-friends. I didn't know what to say, so to fill the space, I said, "Hailey Joanne Pinkey!"

And she said, "Mango Delight Fuller, I was just kidding. Goofing. Relax, mon amie! My parents are renewing their vows, that's what the wedding is about. Didn't your dad tell you? He's doing the catering."

"He is?"

"Trust and believe, my parents wouldn't use anyone else. But the important thing is, we'll be in New York together. Très fantastique, n'est ce pas?"

"Yes, it's fantastic and uber crisp!" I guessed I was getting the hang of French through osmosis. We disconnected, promising to meet up in New York and spend lots of time together.

In spite of all my worries, I fell asleep just before the sun came up. I didn't leave my bed until almost noon. Dada was on a phone call when I stumbled into the kitchen on my way to the bathroom. When I came out, bladder empty, face splashed, and teeth brushed, he was wrapping up his phone call. "Okay, great. It's a deal. Thanks so much. Peace."

I was about to ask him about catering the Pinkeys' vow-renewal, but I was sidetracked by the way he was beaming at me. I knew Dada was up to something. He called out to Mom, "Hey Margie, it's all set!"

Mom hurried into the room with Jasper toddling behind her. "Really? I can't believe it. On such short notice?"

"Toldja I'd get it done."

I was kind of tired of feeling like I'd walked in on the middle of a sitcom. "What's going on? What got done? What's all set? What?!"

44

Dada grinned. "Your mom and I are throwing you a bon voyage party at the community center tomorrow evening!"

Mom chimed in, "You can invite all of your friends from the play."

"No! No-no-no-no!" A party was the last thing I wanted, especially when I had to tell all my friends the bad news that they weren't going to New York, too.

Mom's fists went to her hips. "What do you mean, no? We thought you'd be happy."

"Happy? I'm not happy. I don't want a party!"

Dada crinkled his eyes. "But I've already arranged it with the community center. We can't back out now. I've drawn up a menu and everything."

"That's right, Mango. So give me a list of all your castmates' email addresses so I can get the invitations out ASAP."

"But you didn't ask me if I wanted a party!"

Mom threw her hands up in the air. "Who in their right mind doesn't want a party? Everybody wants a party!"

Before I could answer her, there was a knock at the door and Mom went to answer it. I was about to plead my case to Dada about canceling the party, until I heard . . .

"Oh, hello, Isabelle. Come on in."

Just when you thought things couldn't get worse, things had a way of proving you wrong. Very wrong.

I got dressed and took Izzy to the park to break the news to her, because I didn't want to add to her humiliation by having her break down and cry in front of my parents. But Izzy didn't cry. In fact, she hardly reacted at all. As I reached across the bench to touch her hand and console her, she stood up and smiled. It was a real hard and painful smile, the smile of someone who had never learned how. Sort of like if Professor Snape ever tried to smile.

"Don't worry about it, Mango. I'm a big girl. I'll just let the gang know we're not wanted. It's no biggie. Besides, my cousin Carmella from Texas wants to come visit me this summer, and I haven't seen her since I was five. We were so tight back then! Anyway, now I won't have to disappoint her by not being here. All's well that ends well, huh? Have fun in New York. See ya."

With that, she turned and hurried out of the park. I wanted to go after her, but then again . . . the Snape face kept me right where I was, wondering what was wrong with me. How did I make such a mess of our friendship so fast? Why was I always so afraid of causing trouble that I wound up in an avalanche of trouble?

I thought back to what Hailey Joanne had said. She was right about me. I had to learn to be more direct and in order to do that, I had to become a stronger, less fearful Mango. But right now, I had a lot of planning and packing to do. And more importantly, I had to put a stop to the party.

I got up from the park bench and headed home, but I

was too late. Mom had found my contact list and emailed invitations to all the cast and crew. There was no turning back now. All I could do was get ready to be the guest of honor at a party filled with smiling Snapes.

I didn't think things could get worse . . . but they did.

CHAPTER SIX

It's My Party and I'll Cry If I Want To

BON VOYAGE! Those were the words on the multicolored sign hanging above the door of the community center party room. Dada had called in a favor from his friend at the printer that had made business cards for his catering company, Delicious Delight. He used my middle name, Delight, in his company name, because he believed that if it weren't for me and the situation with Brooklyn, which led to her dad firing him from his restaurant, he wouldn't be in business for himself—and doing very well, by the way.

BOO-LOOP.

There it went–the alert on my phone whenever I got a text. Dreading another cancellation, I tapped on the message icon, and read:

P | sorry mango can't make it today have a nice trip

Yeah, right. *Have a nice trip.* This cancelation text didn't even make up a lame excuse, like the twenty-nine other texts

48

from my other "friends." As excuses went, there were some
pretty spectacular ones, like:

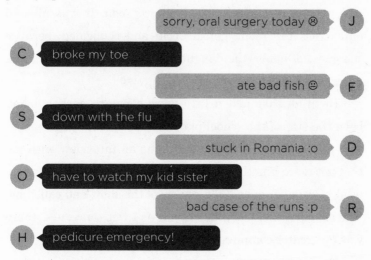

sorry, oral surgery today ☹ — J

C — broke my toe

ate bad fish ☺ — F

S — down with the flu

stuck in Romania :o — D

O — have to watch my kid sister

bad case of the runs :p — R

H — pedicure emergency!

Seriously, "pedicure emergency?" Did his toenails grow
twelve inches overnight or something? I couldn't believe
all my friends from the play would turn on me like this.
Especially since I didn't mean to make such a mess of things.
But the texts had been coming nonstop since six o'clock. My
party was supposed to start at seven, and now it was almost
eight o'clock and I was slumped in a folding chair, glaring at
the happy, optimistic banner that I wanted to rip down and
tear to shreds.

Dada and Mom were standing across the room, trying not
to look at me, their friendless daughter, with pity. It really
sucked, because I knew they'd spent seventy-five dollars to
rent the space and about two hundred on food and drinks.

Dada had been up all night making five different kinds of pizza bites, veggie and curried beef patties, coconut shrimp, and gallons of his famous blueberry soda. It was all laid out across the room, getting cold and congealed, because the guest of honor, the daughter they were so proud of, was officially the most unpopular girl in town.

To think that just a little over a month earlier, I had been the star of the school play and the most popular girl at Trueheart. The school blog had done an interview with me that got more hits than any other post the whole year, and a local newspaper even did a review of the show and called me "the next Beyoncé!" My idol! As far as I was concerned, there was no greater compliment possible.

My friends, the dramanerds—that's what they called us theater kids behind our backs at school, but we owned it and liked it—had started calling me "Baby Bey," and the name caught on all over the school. At the end of the year, I was invited to graduation parties for ninth graders! Seriously, that was like so totally four-leaf clover rare for a seventh grader like me to be invited. And it was all because of the play.

BOO-LOOP.

I checked my phone

 sorry. gargoyle pimple cant be seen in public D:

That was just weak! Hurt feelings were welling up behind my eyes. Luckily, I was saved from a blubbering fest by my little brother, Jasper, who toddled up to me and bopped to the beat of the songs on my summer playlist. It was a mix of pop, hip-hop, R&B, and alternative rock. I got into alt-rock because of TJ. We became really close while rehearsing and performing. He was Romeo and I was Juliet, and I guess the feelings from the show kind of blurred over into real life for a little while. Especially since we had to kiss in the play.

Anywho, he was in an alt-rock band called the Halfrican Americans (because all the members were of mixed race), and he had turned me on to so much cool music that I had never really given a chance before. It was all I'd been listening to this summer. Izzy swore I was only into alt-rock because I missed TJ, but that was not true. He was a friend-friend, not a boyfriend. Someone I used to like-like, but didn't anymore. NOT my boyfriend at all. I hadn't had one of those yet, and with the way this party was turning out, it seemed like I never would.

Oh man, I knew this was going to be the talk of the summer. The party no one came to. Even though I was worried about leaving town and missing my friends and family, right at that moment I couldn't wait to get on that plane in the morning. I wouldn't have to show my shame face around town, and maybe when I got back everyone would have forgotten how and why they all shunned me.

Jasper was getting down right in front of me doing something that could be called breakdancing. He'd learned it from all those times Dada tried to relive his glory days, spinning on his head on the kitchen linoleum. Jasper's moves were hysterical, and I couldn't help but laugh. Mom and Dada clapped and chanted, "Go Jasper! Go Jasper! Go Jasper!"

I joined in. We all moved toward the center of the dance floor, where Jasper was really cutting loose. Dada took my hand and spun me around. I was laughing even harder now. Mom and Jasper paired off, so Dada and I got our own groove going, and for a few blissful moments, I forgot all about being an outcast and surrendered to the beats that filled the dance floor.

When the song ended, Dada hugged me and I noticed someone standing at the door, smiling. It was TJ! I didn't think he would be here. The Halfrican Americans had a gig out of town that weekend, an actual legitimate excuse I had known about before Mom hijacked my contact list and emailed invitations.

It was so coincidental that one of his band's songs came on while he was standing at the door—"*Shallow Skin*," one of my favorites. It was about fitting in with people who were on the other side of popular and being happy about it. We walked toward each other across the dance floor.

"What are you doing here? What happened to your gig?" I asked.

"Long story. All I'll say is the check bounced, and so did we."

"Oh, I'm sorry." I gave him a hug.

"It's cool," he said "I'm glad, 'cause I got to come here." He looked around the room and asked, "Am I early? Where is everybody?"

I opened my mouth to tell him, but I didn't know what to say. The truth was way too painful. And now, at the most inconvenient of inconvenient times, all the feelings that had been piling up behind my eyeballs pushed their way free, and I became a blubbering mess, crying into TJ's shoulder.

By the time TJ's song had finished playing, I had stopped crying. We went outside. The evening air was humid, but there was a bit of a breeze. Sitting on the low wall outside the community center, I spilled my tale of misery and woe. When I finally got the guts to look at TJ to see if he was mad like the rest of the cast, I saw his kiwi green eyes were flashing with anger.

"That's so not cool. So not fair."

"What's not fair? That the whole cast isn't going?"

"No! That they're all blaming you. What could you do about it? I mean, it's not a school play anymore. It wouldn't be realistic to have kids playing our agents or our parents or any of the other roles." He stood up. "I'll be right back. Meet you inside." He walked off, pulling his phone from the pocket of his jeans.

I was happy TJ was on my side, but where was he going? Now, once again, no one was at my party except my parents and baby brother, who was still bopping away when I stepped back into the party room.

My phone BOO-LOOPED, but I refused to look at it. I didn't need, want, or care to see another lame excuse about why no one could come to my going-away party. My phone

BOO-LOOPED again. And again. I asked Mom if I could put it in her purse until we got home. Every BOO-LOOP hurled me farther down into a pit of depression. And that text notification was beginning to wear on my nerves—I'd have to change it sooner rather than later.

I walked by the table, avoiding Dada's eyes. He was pretending to look upbeat, but there was a sadness underneath that he couldn't hide. I grabbed a mini-pizza, shoved it in my mouth, walked to the other side of the room, and sat in one of the empty folding chairs. Then I turned toward the wall, refusing to look at the streamers that were beginning to droop.

Was I really being selfish for going to New York without the rest of the cast? I was so excited about the possibility of going when Bob first offered me the chance that I had completely forgotten about Izzy and her tres leches. If that wasn't being selfish, what was? Izzy and I had been having so much fun hanging out together the first week of summer vacation. Also, if I weren't around to hang with Izzy, how would Jasper get his Izzy fix? He would probably spend his days pining for his super crush, carrying her photo, and mourning the loss of his first love. Having his heart broken at such a young age could scar Jasper for life!

I was beginning to change my mind about New York when TJ returned. He walked straight up to me and said, "Hey, I'm sorry for walking away like that. But what you told me really ticked me off, and sometimes I just need to, you know, walk it off before I get super Hulkish."

"I didn't know you had a temper."

"Everybody has one if they're pushed far enough."

"I guess . . ."

"Listen, you should be mad too, instead of blaming yourself. I mean, look at all the trouble your family went through to set this party up! And now just because you're taking advantage of an opportunity that most of them would give their right frontal lobe for, you're being treated like a piranha."

I couldn't help myself; I started to giggle.

"What's so funny?"

"You said I was being treated like a piranha."

"Right. Like they're shunning you or something."

"I think you meant pariah. A piranha is a fish. The kind of fish that eat flesh and stuff. A pariah is a person who is shunned."

I think I actually saw pink flush in TJ's cheeks. He turned away quickly, then turned back, and we both burst out laughing. Jasper toddled over and started laughing too, which made all of us laugh even harder.

"Mango!" Dada called out.

"Yes?" I turned to him, wiping away my tears of laughter.

Dada pointed to the door, and there stood Boss Chloe, the stage manager of *Yo, Romeo!* A bunch of other kids from the show were there, too. I went from shunned to stunned in one second flat!

Boss Chloe strode over to me, followed by everyone else. "Hey . . . uh . . . sorry about not showing up before. That was straight up rude-ology."

"Yeah," said Hiram, the boy who had played my father in the play. "I'm two months younger than you. No one would believe I was your father in the play for real."

Boss Chloe gave TJ a playful but powerful shove. "Thanks for shame-texting us. You really made me see things from Mango's side."

I looked at TJ, who was rubbing his chest. "Shame-text?"

"Yeah, when I walked away from you before, I sent a group text to everyone setting things straight. Didn't you read it?"

"No . . . I put my phone away, because I thought I was getting more excuse texts!"

Hiram said, "I sent you a text saying sorry, I didn't need a pedicure after all, and I was on my way."

I laughed and noticed more kids from the show coming in the door. I couldn't believe it. Dada started passing around trays of food, and before I knew it, we were all eating and dancing, and it was a real party. I was having the greatest time ever, except for one little thing. Izzy wasn't there.

When the party was almost over and Izzy still hadn't come, I got my phone from Mom's purse to see if she had texted me, but she hadn't. I guessed she was still angry. Or maybe jealous. Or hurt. Or busy hanging out with her cousin Carmella. I had to figure out a way to win my friend back, because come September, life in school without Izzy as a friend would be miserable. I would start thinking about what to do tonight. Or tomorrow, on the plane.

TJ stayed to help us clean up after everyone else left. "By the way, did Bob tell you who was going to play Romeo?" TJ asked, when we were finally done and walking out of the community center.

Uh-oh. Now it was TJ's turn to feel left out. "Um . . ." I hesitated. "Actually, he said he wasn't sure. When he was at my house, he said they were waiting to hear back from some actor, but they were pretty sure he was on board."

"Did he say who?"

"No. He was kind of secretive about it. I wish it was you."

"Well, *alla kazoom, alla kazam*, your wish has come true."

I stopped walking and turned to him. He was smiling and his kiwi green eyes were twinkling under the streetlights.

"What do you mean?"

"I mean, I'm going to play Romeo opposite you again!"

I pushed him a lot harder than I intended to. "SHUT UP!"

"Ow! What is it with girls and shoving? I thought you'd be happy."

"Happy! I'm . . . I'm . . ." I couldn't find the words, so I just threw my arms around his neck and before I knew what I was doing, I had kissed him on the lips. Longer and harder than I ever had when we were in the play. My heart was beating so fast, I couldn't believe I had just done that.

"Mango!"

I leapt away from TJ and turned to see Mom, her eyebrows lifted to her hairline.

TJ, a look of sheer terror in his eyes, said, "See you in New York!" and took off down the street.

"What was that about?" Mom said, walking up to me.

"TJ just told me he was going to New York to play Romeo again. I guess I was just shocked and . . . happy?" I had just thrown my arms around his neck and kissed him. Who did that? Who did that to a boy who was just a friend? He *was* just a friend-friend . . . right? I was confused and embarrassed and feeling feelings I thought I didn't feel.

Mom took out her phone and started tapping out a text.

"What are you doing?"

"Texting your Aunt Zendaya. I just came up with a few more rules to keep you in check while you're away."

CHAPTER SEVEN

Up, Up, and No Way!

TJ and I texted back and forth a bunch later that night.

M why didn't you tell me before?

didn't get a chance **T**

M what about the band?

taking a summer break **T**

M ur parents r ok with it?

they r happy i'm going **T**

M where r u staying

with mr ramsey and his wife. **T**

M I'm so happy

me 2 **T**

who r u staying w/ **T**

mango? **T**

hey? **T**

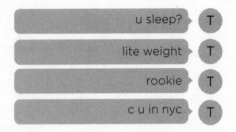

I guessed I kind of fell asleep while we were texting. I scrolled through my texts next morning with a silly smile on my face, giddy that I'd have a friend from Trueheart in New York with me the whole time. (Of course that was the only reason I was smiling.)

It was Sunday morning, and the sun was streaming in through the blinds as I leapt out of bed. I lifted one of the slats, the way Mom always told me not to, and looked out at my street. The buildings across the way, the sad little trees that lined the curb along my block . . . I didn't know what it was, but all of a sudden I was starting to feel this hollowness in my stomach, like what had been inside me was scooped out.

I backed away from the window and looked around my room: my desk, the swivel chair, my bed, the life-size poster of my BCF Gabriel Faust hanging on the inside of my closet door. My nightstand with the lamp and shade I had gotten to choose all by myself for the first time. The family picture we had taken at the JC Penney Portrait Studio a year earlier. Jasper was wearing his Elmo onesie, because he used to burst into tears when he didn't have it on. I smiled, thinking

60

of how Mom had bought three of the same onesies so he didn't smell like sour milk and drool every day of the week. The hollowness in my belly was beginning to expand, and suddenly I knew what I was feeling. I was homesick even before I'd crossed the threshold of my own bedroom.

—

In the car on the way to the airport, the hollowness began to overwhelm me. I had tried to ignore it earlier, but now it was creeping up my skin like moss on tree bark. I could barely force down the special breakfast Dada had prepared earlier of all my favorites: pommes dauphinoise (a fancy French way of saying cheesy scalloped potatoes), his homemade spicy turkey sausage with sage and jerk, gashouse eggs (where the eggs are fried in a piece of toast with a hole in it), and fresh squeezed tangerine and lime juice. I knew he had gotten up early to make this just for me, but I couldn't swallow through the lump that was growing in my throat—because I would miss him so much.

Rolling down the freeway, I turned away from Jasper, who was pointing at all of the cars out the window and identifying them by saying, "Dah! Cah! Dah! Cah!"

How much would he grow in the six weeks I would be away? Would he remember me when I came back? Would I even recognize him? Toddlers grew so fast. I couldn't believe I was going to miss some of those precious moments with him.

FRACASWELL HYMAN

I wished I had an 8 x10 photo of myself that I could frame and give to him, so his memory of me wouldn't be completely replaced by his obsession with Izzy.

My forehead was hot. I felt as though I were getting a fever, so I leaned my face against the cool window. Mom, in the passenger seat, turned around and asked, "Mango? You okay?"

"Uh-huh."

"Why are you sitting there scrunched up like that?"

"I don't know, Mom."

"Dah! Cah!"

"Maybe she didn't eat enough breakfast," Dada said. "I cooked up all her favorites and she just kept moving things around the plate."

"She'll be sorry tomorrow, because she isn't going to get a breakfast like that for a long time," Mom remarked. "Not with Zendaya's 'stick the frozen mess in the microwave and hope for the best' cooking."

Dada chuckled. "I'll never forget the time she blew up the microwave when she called herself cooking Thanksgiving dinner."

"She was heating up the ham still wrapped in foil!" Mom and Dada laughed. The sound of them being so happy together sucked me deeper into a quicksand of homesickness. It was about to pull me completely under and make me change my mind about going.

"Dah! Cah!"

"She set off smoke detectors all over the building."

"The fire department came out on Thanksgiving Day!"

Dada asked, "Didn't Zendaya get engaged to one of the firemen she met?"

"Yeah, but he came to his senses before he let her lure him down the aisle!"

I couldn't take it anymore! I was about to yell, *STOP! TURN THE CAR AROUND! I WANT TO GO HOME!* But we had already arrived at the airport. Dada pulled a ticket from the dispenser, glided into the parking garage, and found a space near the elevator, a stroke of luck that made him start beat-boxing and jerking his shoulders up and down like the fourth place loser in a B-boy dance contest.

Before I knew it, we were at the gate, (my family had arranged to accompany me all the way, since I was a minor), and there, waiting for me, was Bob. He had delayed his own flight to New York so we could fly together and he could deliver me directly to Aunt Zendaya. That was the only way my parents felt comfortable about me flying without them.

Bob opened his long arms and wiggled his jazz hands. "Mango-Mango, are you as excited as I am?"

As he reached for me, well . . . I couldn't help it. I bent forward and hurled special occasion breakfast chunks all over his Crocs. Ugh!

Public humiliation overshadowed everything! Homesickness. Embarrassment. Being misunderstood. EVERYTHING! Public humiliation in an airport, where there were hundreds of people sitting around waiting semi-patiently until it was time to board their flights, with nothing better to do than gawk at Gross Girl from the planet Vomit, was worse than dying of thirst in the middle of the desert with dung beetles crawling all over you. At least, that's what I felt like at that moment.

Mom and Dada assumed I threw up because I was nervous about flying without them for the first time. Bob cracked, "Hey, I know my Crocs aren't as cool as they used to be, but that's no reason to barf all over them." And Jasper, well, I really don't know what Jasper thought, but he clapped and cheered when he saw what I did.

As Bob kind of hopped/limped to the restroom to wash off his Crocs, the airport ticket clerk made an announcement loud enough to be heard on the farthest of Jupiter's 67 moons. "Cleanup at Gate 23. Cleanup at Gate 23. Nervous flyer stomach action." Dada led me to a seat upwind of the foul evidence of my misery. He sat me between him and Mom, who was holding onto the leash attached to Jasper's teddy bear backpack. He was a known wanderer, so the leash helped keep him within five feet at all times.

Dada smiled, wiping my face with his bandanna. "You're going to be okay, Mango gal. The flight is just under three hours. Before you know it, you'll be hugging your aunt and getting ready to be a star."

"I'm not worried about flying."

Mom furrowed her brow. "You feeling sick? Flu? Virus?"

"No! I'm just . . . I'm gonna miss you. All of you."

Dada put his arm around me and hugged me close. "Oh, baby girl, we're going to miss you, too."

Bob came back from the restroom just as they were announcing the boarding for our flight. His Crocs were making a squishy kind of sound, but he said they were a cinch to clean and he couldn't even smell the vomit anymore. Lovely.

My family and I shared the long, tight kind of hug that made it hard to breathe, but I didn't care. I inhaled the coconut butter scent of Mom. I lifted Jasper, whose neck smelled of baby oil and cereal. Dada held me long and hard as I breathed in his natural woody scent mixed in with spices from my special breakfast. As I got in line, I wrapped my hand in Dada's hands, which were calloused and rough from years of chopping, cutting, cooking, and "just growing up a bwoy in the mountains of Jamaica."

It wasn't easy, but finally I let go, had my ticket scanned, and stepped into the tunnel thing that takes you to the door of the plane. The flight attendant was all smiles, greeting us as we boarded.

Bob placed our bags in the overhead bin and insisted I take the window seat. That was very nice of him and very necessary for me, because as the plane took off, I had to turn my face toward the window so he couldn't see the tears rolling down my cheeks.

CHAPTER EIGHT

Aunt Butterfly

Bob had planned on using our time on the plane to go over script changes together, but I slept through most of the flight, my face smooshed up against the window. When I woke up, I had to move, bend, and stretch my neck to remind myself that it was connected to my shoulders. Also, I needed to use the restroom, but Bob, in the aisle seat, was now sleeping— head back, mouth open, long snorting snores sleeping. I tried my best to hold it because I didn't want to wake him, but once my legs started jiggling, I knew it was time to go. So, what did I do? I unbuckled my seatbelt and crawled over him, of course. I kind of felt like Spiderman, the way I stretched my leg across Bob's seat and grabbed onto the seatbelt sign above to steady myself, trying my best not to disturb him.

I succeeded! As I made my way up the aisle, I noticed most people were sleeping or playing games on phones or watching movies. But some glanced up and kind of smirked at me. Some glanced up and gave me a pitying look before quickly turning away. Huh? I thought to myself, *Hey, you could be looking at the next big Broadway star and you don't even know it. One day, you're going to wish you'd asked for my autograph.*

Both restrooms were occupied, so I shimmied a bit as I waited. Finally, one of the doors opened and a little old-fashioned lady came out. I say "old-fashioned" because she was wearing a hat like ladies used to do in old movies. It had a net that covered half her face. She smiled up at me and said, "Oh, you poor dear. You're the girl who threw up in the airport, aren't you? Well, no need to cry. It doesn't matter in the least."

I kind of smiled and nodded, thinking, *Cry? Who's crying, lady?* I went into the restroom, closed the door, and slid the lock into place. Turning to the mirror, I saw why people were giving me odd looks and 1940s grandma thought I was crying. My entire Afro puff was a wreck. It was smashed flat on one side so it looked like I had a flying saucer tilted on top of my head. And my face, OMGZ! My face was streaked with salty, dry tear tracks. Holy mortification! I looked so horrible, I forgot how badly I had to pee and set about washing my face and re-puffing my hair STAT! (That was a little term I learned studying for a medical degree by watching *Grey's Anatomy*.)

The whole situation set me back. I mean, really? One humiliation after another. First, I was the girl who threw up. Then, I was the girl who looked like she crash-landed from another planet. I was so embarrassed, I wanted to spend the rest of the flight in the restroom, but I knew that wasn't possible. So, I thought about what my mom told me to do one time when I was afraid. It happened when I was seven and we lived in a building where the girls who lived downstairs would try to scare me by peeling their eyelids back. Mom told me, "Just because you're afraid doesn't mean your enemy has to know it. Act like you're brave, they'll think you're brave, and then, guess what? You'll *be* brave."

I put on a smile and looked at myself in the cramped mirror. My hair was re-puffed. The tear stains had been wiped away with wet paper towels. I had relieved myself, and so now it was time to leave the restroom. Yes, I was humiliated, but I didn't have to let the rest of the passengers know. If I acted confident, like I thought I was beautiful, then they would think I was confident and beautiful. Right, Mom? It had worked on the bullies when I was seven, and I hoped it would work again now.

I opened the door and walked with my head held high. I moved like a superstar, doing the kind of walk I did when I was playing Juliet, a famous singer winning a Grammy in *Yo, Romeo!* And guess what? No one noticed me, because they were all facing the same direction I was walking. No one could see me, unless they literally had eyes in the back of their head. Oh well.

When I got back to my seat, Bob was waking up. The Fasten Your Seatbelt sign dinged on, and it was almost time to land. I decided I would stick with this confident posture as

I left the plane and came face to face with New York City for the first time since I was five years old.

—

When we got to the baggage claim area, a whirl of color came twirling toward me and Bob—oohing, cooing, and pecking me with kisses and compliments. "Oh my goodness, look at how beautiful you are. Girl, where'd you get them long legs? Look at you! You're way too old to be my niece. We'll have to tell everybody we're sisters. Twins, as beautiful as you are!"

Aunt Zendaya was draped in long colorful robes that looked sort of African and sort of like a Japanese kimono at the same time. The fabric was flowy and covered in swirls of primary colors, and the sleeves were long, like wings. Her head was wrapped in matching cloth, her fingers were covered in jewelry made with wire and colorful stones, long earrings dangled from her lobes, and without a drop of makeup, her skin shone like she had her own personal spotlight following her everywhere she went. As she twirled around to greet Bob, who was staring at her with his mouth open, her sleeves billowed out, and I could have sworn she was a human-size butterfly. Yes, that was it. Aunt Zendaya was a butterfly, and Mom was a moth. Related, but very, very different.

I think Aunt Zendaya was actually flirting with Bob, the way she giggled and lightly touched his arm at everything he said. I believe he was flattered, by the way he blushed and sucked in his stomach. The whole situation was becoming a little awkward, so I was glad when Bob finally left to catch a cab up to Harlem.

As we left the terminal and headed for the garage, Aunt Zendaya went on and on about how much I'd grown since the last time we were together. It was kind of hard to hear her with the sounds of horns honking, traffic, and whistles blowing all around me. I was so busy looking this way and that that I almost walked into the cart loaded with my luggage.

"Do you have a map app on your phone?" Aunt Zendaya asked. She lifted the creaking trunk of what looked like the kind of car you'd see in movies from the sixties, except this one had big rings of rust and the back fender was a completely different color than the rest of the car.

"Is this your car Aunt Z?"

"No, my friend Esteban let me borrow it to pick you up. Isn't it amazing? It's a classic. A relic from the past."

Looked more like a *wreck that wouldn't last* to me, but it wouldn't have been polite to say that. So I just nodded as we loaded my rolling suitcase into the trunk and Aunt Z slammed it shut. The doors creaked as we opened them and took our seats. I was surprised to see that the seat belt fastened across my lap, like the one on the airplane. I was used to seat belts that crossed my chest. I must've been frowning or something, because Aunt Zendaya asked, "Is something wrong, sweetie?"

"Uh, no . . . I was just wondering if this car was safe."

"Honey, this car has been running since before both of us were born, and that says something." She turned the key in the ignition and after a wheezing protest, the car rumbled to a start. Then she flicked a switch and there was a horrible craning sound that made me jump in my seat. When the roof of the car started lifting, I reached for the door handle.

Aunt Zendaya grabbed my arm, laughing, and said, "Haven't you ever ridden in a convertible before?"

As the horrible noise continued, I turned and watched the top as it creaked and groaned down into a space behind the back seat.

"All right!" shouted Aunt Zendaya. "Let's get it, let's go!"

The car glided smoothly out of the parking lot, and it was pretty cool seeing JFK airport from a car without a roof. Aunt Zendaya went on and on about how happy she was that we would get to spend six whole weeks together, how many things there were to show me, how much we had to talk about and learn about each other. While I was interested in everything she had to say, my eyes were so busy taking in all there was to see that I could barely keep up. All at once, my regular old summer vacation had turned into a real adventure!

CHAPTER NINE

All Kinds of People, All Kinds of Kooky

I didn't mean to be ungrateful or snobbish or critical, but living with Aunt Zendaya was going to take some getting used to. For one thing, studio apartments in Brooklyn were beyond small. I mean, her kitchen was the size of Mom's bathroom back at home. There was one kinda-sorta large room that had two windows looking out onto the brick wall of the building next door. One side of the room was Aunt Zendaya's jewelrymaking workspace. There were large spools of gold and silver wire, and boxes on top of boxes, filled with what she called "semiprecious stones" but looked like polished rocks to me. I went to the only other door and opened it, expecting to see a bedroom, but it was just a closet-size bathroom. Actually, there was no bath in the room, just a shower, a toilet, and the smallest sink I had ever seen. Someone had worked really hard to squish everything in there.

I asked, "Where do you sleep?" She pointed to the sofa. "If you sleep on the couch, where will I sleep?"

She laughed. "Sweet child, it's a futon. By day, it's a couch, and by night, it converts into a bed."

She pulled on a bar, and the futon flattened out into what looked like a queen-size bed. But when it was fully converted, it bumped right up against the workspace table, leaving no room to walk on that side of the room. As I looked around, I didn't notice my hands were on my hips until Aunt Zendaya said, "*Umph*. Standing there with your fists on your hips, you're the spitting image of your mama when she gets all judgy. Are you judging my place, sweet child?"

I dropped my arms immediately. "No! No, of course not, Aunt Z. I think it's really, really . . . crisp! Super crispy with a dash of salt."

"What do you like about it?"

I had to think fast. What did I like? Well . . . "I like that it's . . . I mean . . . you could never get lost in here. Everything is within reach . . . all the time."

She shrugged. "That's New York for you, honey. This building used to have big apartments with three to five bedrooms, but then they split them up into studios and jacked the rent up three times higher than it was for the families who used to live here."

"Oh." I wasn't sure what else to say, so I added, "I like the way all your lamps are covered with scarves. Makes the light real pretty."

"I change the color of the scarves to fit my mood. The orange represents excitement, because you're here for six weeks, and I couldn't be happier. You hungry?"

"Starved!" I sniffed the air. "Something smells great. What's cooking?"

Aunt Zendaya waved her hand as if dismissing the aroma. "Ugh, that's something my neighbors are making. Turns my stomach the way they're always cooking swine or some other meat."

My eyebrows took flight. "You don't eat meat?"

"Oh no. Never! I don't eat meat or any products that come from our animal cousins. It breaks my heart that people would ever eat anything that once had a face. How could you look into the eyes of a cow or hog or even a fish and not feel that there was a soul in there crying for equality, humanity, and fraternity?"

I nodded, wishing I hadn't thrown up the last real people food I'd have for six weeks. If Aunt Z looked into my eyes right now, she'd see a soul crying for some bacon, a burger, a butterfly shrimp. I sighed. "Don't you sometimes wish for a slice of pizza?"

"Oh, I love pizza, but not with cheese. Cheese is made with milk which comes from a cow or goat and so it's off limits. Don't worry, sweet child, you are going to love eating cruelty-free. It will double your energy, cleanse your body, and free your soul from all the tortured energy stored in the fibers of an animal murdered for food."

For dinner we had organic carrot sticks, a really thick, flavor-free, multigrain bread smeared with nut butter, green pea purée soup, and banana chips for dessert. I didn't want to appear ungrateful or disrespectful, so I kept a smile on my face as I cleaned my plate. But lying on the futon next to my aunt, I found myself staring at the ceiling, counting bacon cheeseburgers to help me fall asleep.

—

I didn't know how I slept, but I did and surprisingly well. When my phone alarm started buzzing at seven, I leapt out of bed, excited for rehearsal starting at ten. Yes, I knew I had a couple of hours to kill before my rehearsal escort arrived, but I wanted to be ready. Super ready. The more ready I could be, the less nervous I would be—at least, that was my plan.

Aunt Zendaya rolled over and covered her head with the blanket, so I decided I better tiptoe around while getting ready. As I showered, I ran through my lines. I'd been studying my script since I found out I'd be coming to New York. Yes, I know, Bob told me some of the script had changed, but I didn't think the changes would be very big. Since TJ and I had done the play already, we'd be miles ahead of the rest of the cast. It would be fun helping them learn their lines and dance routines the way Izzy helped me back at Trueheart.

Izzy . . . the thought of her made me regret the way my inability to speak up had put a ding in our friendship. I had to find a way to break through to her. I was determined. I was not about to let my mistake ruin our friendship, not when we were so close to being besties. While eating a slice of the thick bread smeared with nut butter (it didn't taste half bad after

I sprinkled some sea salt on it), I decided I would include her in the whole process by taking pics and short videos of everything whenever I could, so it'd feel like she was there with me. I needed to able to confide in her—and I wanted to hear the latest gossip about how her crush on Hector Osario was progressing.

First thing I did was take a video of Aunt Zendaya's studio. That didn't take very long. I texted it to her saying "tight quarters!", then waited a second to see if the dots would start pulsating to let me know she was texting me back . . . but they didn't.

At nine sharp, the door buzzer went off, harsh and loud. Aunt Zendaya bolted upright from under the blanket. "What the . . . ? What time is it? What's going on?"

"I think that must be Miss Zippy. Bob's sister. She's supposed to pick me up and drop me off for rehearsal. Remember?"

"Ohhhh." She stretched and yawned. "Well, buzz her up. Your mama said I shouldn't let you go with her if she looks untrustworthy."

Miss Zippy moved like a hummingbird in a penguin body. Her name suited her perfectly. She zipped around the studio, breathing hard from the walk up four flights and talking nonstop.

"Holy bananas, your place is twice the size of mine. I mean, what is up with that? How much is your rent, if it's not too nosey of me? I live over a restaurant, so forgive me if I smell like Ling Ho's Chinese Food & Taco Palace. I can't get it out of my clothes. Ohmigosh! Shut up! You're the Precious Stone & Wire Jewelry lady! I've seen you at the farmers' market at Grand Army Plaza. Your stuff is great but too rich for my pockets, if you know what I mean. Where do you get all the stones? Do you have any coffee? My brain doesn't finish loading until after my third cup." That's when she took a breath.

Aunt Z just kind of stared at her and asked, "What time will you be bringing my niece home?"

"Well, rehearsals are over at six, so probably about six-thirtyish, unless we hang with the cast for a bit. I'll text you if we're going to do that. Of course, once we start doing dress and tech rehearsals, we might not get back 'til after midnight or one in the A.M., but that won't be for a few weeks now. So, about the coffee?"

Aunt Zendaya, her eyes wide, gave me a look as she guided Miss Zippy toward the door. "There's a Starbucks two blocks away, near the train station. You all have a good rehearsal." With that, she opened the door, gave me a kiss and a hug, and waved us out of the apartment, quickly closing the door behind us.

We stood in the hall for a moment, kind of awkward. "Aunt Z is not a morning person," I said.

"That's okay. You've got to develop a thick skin living in New York. All kinds of people, all kinds of kooky. Not that your aunt is odd but . . . you know." We headed down the stairs. "Listen, could we meet out front from now on? Hiking up four flights was not a part of our deal. We can have a signal so you know it's me. Like . . . how about short buzz, short buzz, long buuuuuzzzzz, short buzz, long buuuuuzzzzz?"

"Sure, that's sounds fine to me," I said.

Zippy sighed, relieved. "Spectac! Besides, I already walked six blocks to get here and I don't want to get my ten thousand steps in before the day really starts . . . you know?"

"Okay, Miss Zippy, no problem."

"Miss Zippy? Honey, you have got to get way over that. You're making me feel like an old lady and I haven't even hit my mid-twenties yet—oops, I meant my mid-thirties. I gotta get out of the habit of lying to everyone about my age, you know? Anyway, just Zippy is fine."

"Just Zippy" walked really fast. I mean, she was hustling down the street and she could really move. Humidity hugged me like a glove. Everything about Brooklyn was bigger, faster, and louder than what I was used to—the sounds, the smells (some good, some horrific), just everything. Zippy heard a train coming, so we skipped the Starbucks and ran down the stairs into the subway. We didn't have time to get me a MetroCard, so Zippy swiped me through, and I followed close as she rammed herself into the crowded subway car. As the doors slammed shut and the train bolted forward, I held on tightly to a pole. There was no place to sit. I checked out the people around me. They were dressed pretty cool for the most part, in a lot of jeans and black, even in the hot summer. Everyone was looking at their phones or reading or staring off into space, listening to whatever was coming through their headphones. No one was having a conversation or even looking at each other. Even the people that seemed to be together were apart. I turned to say something to Zippy, but she had her headphones on and was scrolling through her phone.

Welcome to New York, I guess.

CHAPTER TEN

The Little Girl in the Mirror

For some rookie reason, I thought we'd be rehearsing in a theater, but Zippy and I zipped into a tall office building and up an elevator to the sixteenth floor. When we stepped off the elevator, I was surprised to see the halls were crowded with dancers in leotards, stretching, and other people I assumed were actors, clutching headshots and mumbling quietly to themselves as they went over lines. The smell of sweat, coffee, and dust dominated the air. And a mixture of sounds flooded into the hall: piano-playing, singing, dance instructions, "One two three, one two three, plié, jeté!" I was so busy taking it all in, I kept walking when Zippy stopped at the door with "STUDIO H" on it. "Mango!" she said, waving me over. "We're in here."

I hurried back to Zippy and entered a room with about forty people. Bob and Mr. Ramsey and three or four other people were seated behind a long table in front of a mirror. When Bob saw me, he stood, clapping his hands for attention

80

and calling out, "Ladies and gentlemen, our star has arrived!"

I turned to see whom he was talking about, but the applause quickly made me realize it was me! I didn't know what it was, but my heart started beating really fast and my breath came in short gasps and suddenly I felt like I wanted to cry. Mr. Ramsey hurried over and gave me a hug, which was really weird because he was always so formal. I mean, he *was* the kind of teacher who always wore a suit jacket and tie, and here he was in jeans and a LOVE IS LOVE T-shirt. "A bit overwhelming, huh?" he whispered in my ear. I nodded into his shoulder, and he led me to a space in a corner of the room.

He sat me down in a chair and took the seat next to me. "Listen, Mango, we're thrilled to have you here. You are going to be great in this production. Don't let yourself be intimidated because you don't know anyone yet. You'll all become a family pretty soon, the same way you did at school. Okay?"

I nodded, trying to push down the urge to bite my fingernails. Around the room, everyone went back to what they were doing—talking in groups, stretching, looking at their phones. I could see that my arrival was a much bigger deal to me than it was to any of them.

I saw myself in the mirror that covered the entire wall. I looked like a frightened little girl compared to all the other cast members in the room. The women were in sporty yoga pants and tops or leotards that hugged their curves. Some of them were wearing make-up and had hair extensions and stylish haircuts. I knew I shouldn't compare myself to anyone, but right then and there, I did not feel like the star of a show. I just felt like a kid.

Things started to come back into focus when I saw TJ ambling across the floor toward me. What a relief! I was happier than ever that he was also in the play. At least we had each other in this sea of strangers—professional actors, singers, and dancers who would be judging us to see if we were worth bringing to New York.

Mr. Ramsey went back to the table, and TJ took his seat. We quickly reached for each other's hands. He squeezed mine and said, "Did you know onions are poisonous to cats?" I laughed. Here we go again with obscure factoids. I guessed TJ was nervous too, because he always came out with these weird things when he was feeling off balance.

At exactly ten o'clock, Bob called for everyone's attention. He introduced the producers, the designers, and our stage manager, Acorn Cao, a super-tall Asian guy with a blond man-bun. Then Bob began talking about the show, a modern day *Romeo and Juliet* set in the music industry of the nineties, the rehearsal and performance schedule, and how excited he and Mr. Ramsey (who was now Larry to everyone) were to bring their first collaboration to New York. "We're very proud of this show, and I'm sure that if each and every one of you pours your heart and soul into this production, we'll all have jobs on Broadway by next spring!" Everyone applauded. We went around the room, introducing ourselves and our roles or jobs, and then it was time to get down to work. First up, the table read of the script.

Things were going along pretty well . . . except for me not speaking loud enough and mumbling through a LOT of unexpected new dialogue. When it was time for my first song, Bob asked me to get up and sing. I was uber nervous, but I went to stand next to Mr. Ram—I mean, Larry—at the piano. He began to play the intro, and just as I opened my mouth, Beyoncé started singing, "Who run the world? Girls." It was my ringtone! How embarrassing! Some of the cast laughed and some groaned. I was not making a good first impression.

I ran across the room to shut my phone off, but when I picked it up, I saw it was Mom face2facing me. Uh-oh . . . I had forgotten to call her this morning. I had promised I'd check in every morning, but with everything new coming at me, I had completely forgotten. I couldn't just reject the call. I turned to Bob and said, "Sorry, it's my mom." Some people giggled, others rolled their eyes, and Bob told everyone to take five.

After a minute of chewing me out for forgetting my promise to call every morning, I spoke with Mom, Dada, and Jasper, too. I gave them a quick face2face tour of the rehearsal space, then stepped out into the hall before mentioning how nervous I was and how I was having second thoughts about being here.

"Well, you're there now," Mom said, "so just call up some

courage, even if you have to fake it, because you committed and you can't back out now, baby."

I should have known Mom would not be sympathetic to my worries. But she was right. All I could do was buckle down and do my best. After hanging up, I went back to the piano and sang my first solo, *"Giving Him a Piece of My Heart."* At the end of the song, the whole cast and crew cheered, and all at once, I felt the warmth of their welcome. I was glad to be right where I was at that moment in time.

When TJ and I did our song, *"Duet Forever,"* it seemed like the deal was sealed. Everyone in the room agreed that we deserved to be there among them.

CHAPTER ELEVEN

Crushed by My Crush

At lunch, Bob treated me and TJ to our first slices of real New York pizza. Now, there was a *New York–style* pizza place where I lived, but it was nothing like *real* New York pizza. The sauce, the cheese, the easily foldable pizza crust, and the oil dripping from it, OMGZ! It was a slice of heaven—pun intended. Just as we were getting comfortable, talking in between bites about how exciting it was to be in New York, Bob got an emergency text from Larry and said he had to head back to the rehearsal studio right away.

TJ and I stayed and finished our pizza and geeked out about how cool it was to be here together, working with professional actors and having lunch breaks like it was a real job—and getting paid!

At one point, we ran out of things to talk about. There was an awkward silence. As I took a sip of my bottled water, I could feel TJ's beautiful kiwi-green eyes watching me, and I didn't know why, but I felt shy all of a sudden. Trying to look casual and cool and NOT think about the kiss, I took another bite of my pizza. A long, gooey string of cheese would not let go as I put the slice down. TJ reached across the table with a plastic knife and sliced through the cheese. That kind of lifted the cloud of awkward, and we took a selfie together biting into our slices. I immediately texted it to Izzy, tagging it with #worldsbestpizza. I waited for the dots to appear saying she was writing back, but they didn't come. Ugh.

TJ and I made our way back to the studio without getting lost, and as soon as we walked in, I could tell something was up. Something was wrong. Very wrong. Bob, Mr. Ram—uh, Larry—and the producers were huddled at their table in deep conversation. Bob and Larry seemed pretty upset, and it got me wondering if the show was being canceled. I went over to Zippy and asked, "What's going on?"

She shrugged. "Beats me. But whatever it is, from the looks of my brother, when his face is as red as his hair, it's not good. Not good at all."

Acorn told everyone to take ten, even though we'd just gotten back from lunch. As we were heading out of the room, Bob asked TJ to stay behind. It was weird that TJ was being singled out. I looked at him and smiled, not wanting to seem worried, but from the look in his eyes, I don't think he bought it.

Waiting in the hall, a bunch of the other actors came over to introduce themselves and say how great they thought my voice was and how TJ and me singing together was mega-amazing. Cartier—one name—the choreographer who had tattoos all the way down both of her arms, said, "Listen, not to worry you, but the dances are going to be a lot more challenging than what you may have done in middle school. But I got you. You look great, I look great. You look awkward, I look like a loser, and I am NO loser." I smiled and nodded as the toes on my two left feet spasmed in my sneakers.

The actress who was playing the queen (aka Juliet's—my—mom) was a regal black woman with long, auburn braids that went all the way down to the small of her back. She came up to me and said, "Hi. We haven't been properly introduced, I'm afraid. My name is Rosalind Windemere, but you can call me Roz."

"Hi. I'm Mango. Nice to meet you."

Her eye narrowed. "Nice to meet you, too. Even nicer to be working. I don't mean to pry, but how old are you, child?"

"I'm twelve. Twelve and a half."

All of a sudden, Zippy was next to Roz. "Looks like she could be ten, or nine even!"

"That's good," Roz said. "I didn't want to be playing the mother to some teenager. I don't mean to brag, but I don't look old enough to permanently move into 'mother' roles yet, know what I mean?"

Zippy cackled. "You don't have a thing to worry about, Roz. This child hasn't even started developing. No one would ever suspect she was a teen."

Roz leaned closer to Zippy. "I started, you know, developing when I was ten. It's a good thing she's on the slow train, 'cause if she looked like I did at twelve, I would've turned this part down." Roz and Zippy laughed and walked off.

Slow train? My eyes were stinging, and my cheeks were hot. They were throwing shade at me, right in front of my face, as if I weren't even there! I felt more self-conscious about looking like a kid than ever. What was I doing here? These were grown-ups. New Yorkers. At least I had one real friend here. I was going to stick close to TJ—like butter on toast.

Acorn called us back into the studio and had us take seats in front of the producer's table. I could tell we were in for some bad news, because Bob was now even redder than his hair. After a moment, he stood to address us.

"Listen, we all know how magical show business is. I mean, that's why we're here, right?" He ran his fingers through his hair and paused to look at Larry, who gave him a small nod. Bob turned back to us. "The best way to say this is just to say it. It's sad on the one hand, and I guess it's good on the other. Well . . . here it is: TJ is being replaced. He will no longer be playing Romeo."

There was a big GASP and everyone turned to look in my direction. Was it just me? I was beyond shocked. I mean, having TJ in the show was the best part of being here. He was my only ally. What would I do without him? I looked around the room and realized he wasn't there.

"TJ left early," Bob said. "He's got some thinking to do and decisions to make and . . . well, he's a strong kid. We all know how talented he is. I mean, you all heard him sing this morning, right?"

There was a rumble of voices agreeing and someone shouted, "Let's give it up for TJ!"

The room burst into applause. I was late on the uptake, because I was crumbling on the inside. Less than an hour ago, we had been celebrating how lucky we were, and now I could just imagine how devastated TJ must feel. This was the worst thing that could happen. Suddenly, I didn't care what Mom had said about sticking it out. I didn't want to be here anymore. I was going to quit. The production went back on its promise to TJ, so why should I have to honor my promise to them? Yeah! As far as I was concerned, I was out of there.

The ovation for TJ wound down, and Bob continued. "Anyway, I guess you're all wondering who TJ's replacement is going to be. Well, we'd actually contacted this actor at the start of casting and it seemed he was unavailable, but he has cleared his schedule and is available now. Also, because he is joining the production, our producers have agreed to add another ten thousand dollars to our publicity budget. So, we should all be grateful that our new Romeo will be none other than Gabriel Faust."

SHUT UP! Gabriel Faust? THE Gabriel Faust? My BCF since fifth grade and the life-size poster hanging on the inside of my closet door? I would actually get to meet him in person. Work with him. Play Juliet to his Romeo. KISS HIM! OMGZ!!!

Suddenly, I felt like I was falling, even though I was sitting criss-cross applesauce on the floor. Maybe it was because two opposite feelings were crashing into me at the same time. Number one, I was distressed because my friend had been replaced, and number two, I was ecstatic because I was going to get up close and personal with my favorite star in the world . . . after Beyoncé, of course. I lay back on the floor, my eyes filled with tears. Of sorrow? Of joy? I really couldn't tell. Maybe sorrow in the left eye and joy in the right?

CHAPTER TWELVE

A View from the Brooklyn Bridge

Rehearsal ended early because our new star wouldn't arrive in New York until tomorrow morning. Also, everyone was shell-shocked by the news. At least, I was. I guessed nobody else really knew TJ. They didn't know how nice he was, how funny, how weird he could be with the factoids that popped out of his mouth when he was nervous.

Bob came over to talk to me right after Acorn dismissed everyone. "Listen, I know you're upset about TJ not playing Romeo this time, but we've offered him a chance to understudy Gabriel. That way he'd get to spend the summer here in New York and hang out with the company and you."

I tried my best to smile. "Is he going to do it?"

"I don't know yet. He said he'd sleep on it and let us know." Bob ran his hand through his cockatoo crown of red hair. "To be perfectly honest, Larry and I didn't want to make this change, but . . . Gabriel is a big star. Or at least he was a couple of years ago. He has over eleven million followers on social media, and that's important to the producers. It gets butts in the seats, and he can promote the show and possibly get us some press and reviews from the important critics."

I could tell Bob felt really bad about TJ. I did too, but I didn't want to make Bob feel worse by showing him how sad I was so I decided to do a little acting for the first time that day. "Bob, don't worry about it. I'll talk to TJ tonight, and he'll understand. Besides, next to Beyoncé, Gabriel Faust is my favorite star. *Brat House* was my favorite show when I was a kid. I mean, I'm still kind of a kid, but when I was really a kid, like seven or eight . . . you know?"

Bob smiled, gratefully. "That was one of the most popular shows on TV back then. He played um . . . what was his name?"

"Romper."

"Yeah, that's right. Romper. What was his catch phrase? That thing he used to say on every episode?"

"Brats rule, fools drool!"

"Yeah, that's right. Brats rule, fools drool. . . I still don't know what the heck that means."

"Me neither, but he was awfully cute when he said it. I had the biggest crush on him."

Bob's eyebrows levitated to his hairline. "Oh really?"

Did I say that out loud? I felt heat rising to my cheeks. I needed to backtrack. "I HAD a crush. Back when I was a kid. I don't anymore! I mean, I had a life-size poster of him hanging in my closet and everything. I loved his music too, but now I'm

more into alt-rock. His songs were so bubblegum, you know?"
I was babbling. I always did this when I was embarrassed,
pulling out the stops to pretend I wasn't embarrassed in the
first place. It never worked and I knew it, so I just stopped
talking.

Bob laughed. "Okay. . . So, one question: do you still have
the life-size poster hanging in your closet?"

"No! I mean, yes, it's still there. But I don't look at it or
practice kissing with it anymore." Oh no! Did I say that out
loud, too? ARRRRGGGGHHHHH! I was ready to dissolve
into a pile of steaming humiliation. Thank goodness Zippy
chose that moment to come up and save the day!

"Hey, kiddo, it's such a nice day out, and we're leaving
early. What say we walk back to Brooklyn?"

"Huh? Walk?"

"That's a great idea," Bob said. "It'll give you a chance to
see more of the city."

"But isn't there a river between here and Brooklyn?"

"Yeeeeaaaah." Zippy stretched the word out like sarcasm-
flavored taffy. "We also have these things in New York called
bridges. Cars and trains ride over them, and some of them
even have separate sections for people to ride bikes or just
use their feet."

Bob put his arm around my shoulder and walked us
to the door. "Don't mind her, she was born salty. It'll be fun
walking across the Brooklyn Bridge!"

"More importantly, I'll get my ten thousand steps in,"

Zippy said, pointing to the tracker she wore around her wrist. "Gotta get in shape for my big number, right, bro?"

Bob rolled his eyes. "Right, Zippy, it's all about you, sis."

Our stage manager, Acorn, met us at the door and handed me my script. "Don't forget this. We'll do a full cast read tomorrow. I'll text you your call time. See ya!" I waved and headed to the elevator with Zippy.

Out on the street, Zippy zoomed in, out, and around the surge of people on the sidewalk. Everyone here was moving so fast, and Zippy could definitely be a contender if the Olympics ever gave gold medals for racewalking. It was lucky I had been a runner on my school's Girls On Track team, because that was the only way I could keep up with her. A part of me didn't want to keep up, though. I still wasn't completely over her joking that I was on the "slow train" of my body developing. I wasn't sure that I could trust her, but since I didn't know how to get home yet, I figured I shouldn't let her out of my sight.

As we zipped through lower Manhattan, Zippy told me her life story and how she had left home at seventeen to come to New York and be a star. "I was the real theater buff in the family. Bobzy caught the bug from me. I used to make him act out scenes from movies with me from the time he could talk! Wouldn't you know it, after all these years of auditions, rejections, odd jobs, and part-time jobs, my little brother is the one who's written the part that's gonna make me a star. I mean, seriously, this came along just in time. I'll be thirty-five in a few weeks, a couple of days after opening night actually. So this is a great birthday present for me, because my time was just about to be up."

"What do you mean?" I asked.

"I mean, I came here when I was seventeen, and I've been chasing my dream for seventeen years. I promised myself that if I didn't make it by thirty-five, I'd face reality and become a civilian."

"Civilian?"

"Yeah, you know, a regular person with a regular nine-to-five job. Show business people are different from regular folk. Most regular people have reliable incomes, secure relationships. Show people like us, we're dreamers. We keep reaching for the stars even if we never get off the ground. Look at that kid today—whatshisname . . . TB?"

"TJ," I corrected.

"Yeah. He probably got his first dose of heartbreak today, but believe me, it won't be his last. You've got to grow a thick skin if you want to be in this business. Anyway, if this show doesn't work out for me, I'm turning in my toe shoes."

"You're a ballerina?"

"Uh, no, not with these hips. It's just an expression, kiddo."

We arrived at the Brooklyn Bridge and joined the stream of people heading across the walkway. When we got to the center, we stopped and looked out at the view. The water shimmered like a million sequins reflecting the sun. The

Manhattan skyline seemed to gleam, too. Zippy held her arms open wide as if she were giving the city a big hug. "Even if I do quit show biz and become a civilian, I'll never leave New York. I fell in love with the city the first time I saw this skyline when I was seventeen. And look at you, you're only twelve and getting your big break. If you are as good as Bobzy says you are, you're gonna be on your way to the big time, and then you'll hold this city in the palm of your hand!"

I shivered at the thought of becoming a star. Then my nerves started to kick in as I started to think about the flip side of this dream. What if I wasn't up to it? I was an amateur. All the other actors in the show had been at it for years. They were all pros, stuck with a nobody like me playing a leading role. How would I feel if I were a big star like Gabriel Faust doing a play with a rookie like me? I turned away from the view and closed my eyes. My head was beginning to spin. I leaned on the railing.

Zippy put a hand on my shoulder. "What's the matter, Mango? You sick?"

"Kind of . . . I just got a little worried, because, well . . . Gabriel Faust is famous and I've only been in one school play. What if he hates working with me?"

Zippy let out a big laugh and clapped me on the back. "Let me tell you something, kiddo. Gabriel Faust *was* a big star. He's not so big anymore. His last two albums flopped, and his comeback TV show only lasted three episodes before it was canceled. He's doing our show because he needs to reboot his career. I mean, really, he's only fifteen and he's a has-been. He should be kissing your feet the way you can sing! Mister Autotune is going to have to bust a gut keeping up with you."

"You think he uses that?"

"Of course! Every singer who can't really sing uses it to sound like they can stay on key."

"But he's had lots of hit records. . ."

"Records, yes, but I bet he lip synchs in concert. All that acrobatic dancing he does, he could never get away with doing those flips and singing at the same time. Wise up, kiddo. He needs this show to be a hit just as much as we do."

As we continued making our way across the bridge, I was still wondering if I should rethink my dream of being in show business. It was cruel the way your hopes could be dashed just like that, the way it happened to TJ today. Suddenly, I was feeling the pressure—way more than anything I had felt when I was doing *Yo, Romeo!* in school. People were counting on this to save their careers, maintain their youthful image, and who knew what else! Could I do it?

I realized I needed TJ to stick around for the summer more than ever. If I was going to have any chance of a future in show business, I also needed this show to be a success, and for that, I needed TJ here by my side. I decided to face2face him as soon as I got back to Aunt Zendaya's. If he was going to sleep on his decision, I had to make sure I was smack dab in the middle of his dreams.

CHAPTER THIRTEEN

Human Toenails

Back in Aunt Zendaya's apartment, I tried making a face2face call to TJ—but no answer. Unavailable. I tried a regular phone call, which went straight to voice mail. I tried texting, but there were no pulsating dots. No response at all! Finally, I tried wooing my friend with one of the things I knew he loved best—an obscure factoid. I quickly googled "weird facts" and found one that was as strange as it was gross. Perfect!

 for $25 u can order a jar of human toenails online

I giggled. That ought to get his attention! I waited. And waited. Suddenly the dots under my text started pulsing. It worked! He'd read my text and was about to answer. Yes! And then . . .

Not 2day. Talk 2morrow.

I was disappointed, but I understood. He must've been really hurting. I should have known. Anyone who could write songs as well as TJ had to be sensitive. So I sent him a couple of heart emojis and let him be.

Izzy was next on my list. It had been almost a week since the *hoof-in-mouth* moment I'd had at McDonald's. But how to approach her? Should I tell her the news about TJ? Would that be gossiping? Maybe I could just tell her Gabriel Faust was going to be in the play and leave the TJ getting replaced part out? But then would she think I was bragging? Izzy had a big-time crush on Gabriel Faust, too. Throwing this info out to her might make her jealous, which would be even worse. So maybe not. There had to be another way. . .

Aunt Zendaya, who was across the room making jewelry, paused to glance at me. "What's got your eyebrows all scrunched up?"

"I'm trying to figure something out."

"Well, you'll never come up with a solution or whatever by giving yourself a brain cramp. Relax. Do something else, and before you know it, a solution will come to you. That's what works for me."

I shrugged. Maybe she was right. I decided to face2face Dada. I could always rely on him and his corny jokes to take my mind off whatever was cramping my brain.

He picked up on the first ring.

"Mango! My sweet breadfruit! We were just picking up the phone to call you!"

"Really? We? We who?"

He reached down to pick up Jasper, sitting him on

his lap. "Me and me brethren here! Say hi to Mango, my youth!"

"Mago! Mago!" Jasper started waving his arms and reached for the phone.

Seeing him tickled me so much, but at the same time, it made me miss him and miss home. Yes, face2face was a great invention, but it could only do so much when you were far away from the ones you loved. I couldn't touch Jasper or squeeze him or kiss his soft peach fuzz cheeks. Suddenly, I got a lump in my throat. "What a gwan, Mango gal?" Dada asked. "You making eye water? Why so?"

"Because, I miss you guys."

"We miss you, too. But we're happy to see you. Right, Jasper?" Dada bounced Jasper on his knee, making him laugh and clap his hands for more.

Aunt Zendaya looked up from her work. "What's going on over there?" She came across the room, looked at my phone, and cooed, "Jasper. Hi, baby! Oh, aren't you the cutest thing I've seen all day!" She shook her head as she went back to her workspace. "That boy could charm the rings off Saturn!"

That was it! I had an idea. A big gesture! I could use my brother to get to Izzy. Well, maybe *use* was not the best word choice. I wasn't actually going to *use* Jasper, but I was going to dangle him like a carrot and see if my girl Izzy would bite. I filled Dada in on my plan, and he agreed to help me out.

I waited until after dinner to call Izzy, which was a good idea, because plotting kept my mind off what my stomach was trying to digest. Aunt Zendaya had made vegan tofu burgers. They didn't taste that bad, actually, but I just wished she wouldn't call them burgers. The word *burger* got my digestive juices flowing in one direction, but the vegetarian tofu part made my taste buds feel like I was playing a trick on them. They weren't as open to the interesting flavor as they would have been if she'd called them, I don't know, maybe *vegan-fu flat round disks?* Anywho, as I said, they didn't taste that bad, but *not that bad* isn't the same thing as *good.*

But back to Izzy. It was time to set my plan in motion. I grabbed my phone and opened my text app, thinking for a minute. I had to word this just right—*these things had to be handled delicately* as the Wicked Witch says in *The Wizard of Oz.* After typing and deleting and typing again and deleting some more, I finally landed on the right words:

Jasper really misses his favorite star. Can dada bring him 4 a visit 2morrow? Please?

I waited. And waited some more. And then . . . pulsing dots! She was answering me. I almost didn't realize I was holding my breath, but it was taking her so long to answer, I started to become light-headed! Just as I let myself breathe, I got a response:

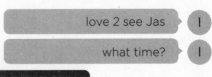

love 2 see Jas

what time?

Dada will call u 2morrow

Okay, so I finally got a response out of her. Now what? The door was open, but just a tiny crack. Could I pry it open more? I decided to give it a shot.

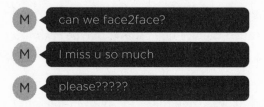

I added a bunch of crying emojis. Then I waited. And waited ... and no response at all. I slumped back on the futon. Then suddenly, my phone started buzzing and vibrating. It was Izzy. She was face2facing me! I accepted the call, and as soon as we saw each other, we both burst into tears and apologies.

We talked for hours. I gave Izzy a tour of the mini-apartment, filled her in on what it was like riding the subway and having rehearsals in Manhattan, and also gave her the deets on what had happened to TJ and how Gabriel Faust was replacing him. This part made her drop her phone while pretending to faint! I laughed so hard my eyes started watering again. I wasn't laughing about TJ, but Izzy was so funny and wild, I couldn't help myself. I was so glad we were talking again.

Finally, around 11, Aunt Zendaya asked me to stand up so she could unfold the futon and we could go to bed. Izzy and

I said goodnight, then I changed into my pajamas and joined Aunt Zendaya under the covers. She was already snoring. Not a harsh bulldozer kind of snore, but more like a little kitten, so it wasn't that bad.

Lying there with the day on replay in my brain, my thoughts floated back to Roz and Zippy laughing about how young they thought I looked. It kind of ticked me off. I was twelve. Why'd they have to act like I was ten or nine? So maybe I wasn't as developed as some other girls, yet. Mom always told me to be patient, and that my time would come. But it was hard being patient when all of my girlfriends were already wearing bras. And now I was surrounded by all these women in rehearsals! I had to do something to at least make myself feel more mature, like I belonged.

Aunt Zendaya didn't wear much makeup, if any at all, but I thought I'd seen a small bag of cosmetics in the bathroom. I tried to get up quietly, but then I immediately banged my shin on the metal bar of the futon. "OUCH!"

Aunt Zendaya lifted her head and without opening her eyes, croaked a groggy, "Huh?" Then her head dropped back onto the pillow. I stood there frozen, until the kitty-cat snoring resumed. Very carefully, I maneuvered myself around the tight furniture and into the bathroom, silently closing the door and turning on the light. I unzipped Aunt Z's makeup bag. There was some mascara, a thing of blush, a pair of false eyelashes that looked like they'd never been used, an eyelash curler, and about six tubes of lipstick in different shades.

With so many lipsticks, I figured it would be hard to miss one tube, and besides, I'd never seen Aunt Z wear lipstick anyway. I studied the colors and decided on a pale, soft pink. That wouldn't be as noticeable as the red, cranberry, or black. Black? Hmm . . .

I crept back into bed, stashing the lipstick under my pillow. Mission accomplished. Starting tomorrow, I wasn't going to be a plain old Mango anymore.

Then my thoughts wound their way back to Izzy. I was so relieved she and I were on the road to being besties again. Or maybe we were besties already? I guessed it was kind of hard to tell when I was so far away from home and we couldn't hang out like we'd been doing at the beginning of the summer. I decided to give our friendship the benefit of the doubt—Izzy was my bestie! Done, did, and decided!

I smiled as I started to drift off. Tomorrow was going to be a big day. First, I'd call TJ and do everything I could think of to make him feel better so he'd stay in New York. Then, I'd get to meet my idol crush, Gabriel Faust. I shivered with excitement. *How lucky could I get?!*

CHAPTER FOURTEEN

Mister Car Tunes

I woke up early, and texted TJ. No response. So I took a shower, then texted TJ. No response. While brushing my teeth, my phone buzzed and vibrated. Yes, it was him! Nope. It was Mom. Even though my mouth was full of toothpaste, she insisted on having a conversation with me before she had to leave for work. I finished talking to Mom, rinsed my mouth and gargled, and texted TJ. No response. I ate a cup of high-protein, low-carb oatmeal, then texted TJ *again*. Still no response. *Ugh*! How could I convince him to stay if he wasn't talking to me?

Just before Zippy picked me up for rehearsal, TJ *finally* responded to my nonstop text messages! He apologized for not answering all of my morning texts, saying it wasn't diva behavior, but he'd had a hard time falling asleep and didn't close his eyes until just before dawn. He agreed to meet me before rehearsal, at the coffee shop next door to the building where we rehearsed. As we emerged from the subway, I turned to Zippy. "I'm going to go to the coffee shop and grab a water. Meet you upstairs!"

Zippy said, "I'll go with. I haven't had my quota today."

Remembering how snarky she was yesterday, I didn't want her there when I met with TJ. "What do you want?" I asked her. "My treat. I'll get it for you."

"Oh, you're sweet, kiddo. Get me a large double shot dyno with steamed milk, whipped cream, and extra cinnamon. Oh, and I'd love a biscotti. Two if it's not too much."

"Sure." I stretched my lips into a sort of smile, already regretting my offer. It wasn't like I had a lot of money to spend. My parents had given me a strict budget of twenty dollars a day, and after paying for my subway rides to and from rehearsal, that didn't leave me a whole lot for lunch, which I had learned was *not* cheap in New York! But it was the price I had to pay for privacy, so I sucked it up.

I spotted TJ right away, even though he was sitting with his back to the door. It was easy to recognize him by his fro-hawk hair. I ordered Zippy's coffee and *one* biscotti, and decided I'd use the water fountain instead of splurging on a bottled water for myself.

I came up behind TJ, carrying the coffee. "Hi."

He turned to me and smiled, but there was a pained look in his eyes. I could tell he wasn't over what had happened, not yet.

"Hi, Mango."

I sat across from him. "How're you doing?"

"Not so great. You know . . ."

"Yeah. It's a total toilet situation."

He smiled. "Nice way to put it."

"So . . ." I took a deep breath. "Are you going to stick around and understudy whatshisname?"

"Come on, Mango, you know his name. Say it."

"I won't."

"Then I will. Gabriel '700 gazillion followers' Faust."

"I'm sorry, TJ."

"Don't be. What they're doing is good business. I barely crack 900 followers. It makes sense for the show. I don't blame Bob or Larry. I just . . . I guess to be completely honest with you and only you, I'm kind of jealous."

"Jealous? Why?"

"Well, he's huge."

"Not anymore. At least, not as huge as he was . . . that's what I heard."

"Yeah, but he's sold millions of records, and I haven't sold any. I don't even have a recording contract."

"But your music is better than his! Deeper and just way cooler. His music is for little kids."

"I bet you downloaded his music. Didn't you?"

"Yeah, but that was, like, a long time ago. I'm much more into your music now."

"Mango, remember when we were backstage at school and you admitted you had a life-size poster of the dude on your wall?"

"Closet door! Inside closet door to be precise."

"Yeah, so this is kind of cool for you, to be acting with your crush. Isn't it? Admit it."

"I'd much rather be acting with you."

"Aw, come on. Let's keep it transparent, okay?"

"Okay, okay! I admit it, it's kind of exciting. But it stinks at the same time. I don't want you to be hurt. We have fun together. And I need you to be here, to keep me sane! I don't want you to go!"

"There's nothing for me to do here. Besides . . ." He leaned in, looked down at his hands and spoke softly, "I'm embarrassed."

"You don't have anything to be embarrassed about."

"Uh, yeah! I just got fired."

"You're not fired. Everybody wants you to stay. The whole cast heard what a great singer you are yesterday. And now we're stuck with Mr. Car Tunes!"

"Huh?"

"Car tunes? You know, the stuff they use when they make records to make sure you sing on key and stuff?"

"I think you mean *autotune*."

"Oh yeah . . . oops."

TJ started laughing, and he suddenly looked so much more at ease, so I started laughing, too. "You are so uber kooky," he said. "That's one of the things I love about you."

Wait a second. Did he just say, *LOVE?* Did my heart just pick up the tempo from a waltz to a trap beat?

108

"Mango, there you are!"

I looked up. Acorn was at the entrance to the coffee shop, carrying a cup holder with four coffees. "Hi," I said.

Acorn held up his watch. "Time. Don't be late."

I nodded. "On my way."

Acorn smiled and left. I leaned back in my seat, not really ready to leave just yet. Had TJ actually said *love* and meant what he said?

I couldn't look at TJ. Not with those kiwi-green eyes. I noticed that my jaw was clamping and my cheeks were getting hot. I was desperate to do something, anything that would make me look less awkward for not looking at him so, in that moment of panic, I picked up Zippy's coffee and took a big long gulp. Then I realized it wasn't my coffee and Mom didn't allow me to actually drink caffeinated coffee yet, and so I sort of coughed and it sprayed out onto the table. Yuck!

TJ's kiwi-greens opened really wide and he looked at me like he was in shock, but at the same time trying hard not to laugh. He was trying too hard. Suddenly, he couldn't help himself and he just burst out LOLing.

I picked up a napkin and wiped the table. He finally stopped laughing. I guess it was because I couldn't even manage to crack a smile. TJ reached across the table and put his hand on mine.

"I'm sorry, Mango. I shouldn't have laughed, but . . . You sure do make me feel better."

I looked at him. "So, you'll stay?"

"I don't know . . ."

"TJ, listen, you should stay because you're in New York! Duh! The music capital of the world. You've got lots of recordings of you and the Halfrican Americans. Maybe you can find an agent or get a record deal or some club dates while you're here."

"I'm here, but my band isn't."

"If you get a gig, they can come. The Halfrican Americans can totally take New York by storm. You can own this city! Come on, what are you waiting for? Think big!"

He looked at his phone. "Actually, what are *you* waiting for? You're late for rehearsal."

I remembered Acorn holding up his watch. "Oops! Gotta go! You should stay. In New York. Okay?"

"You make a pretty good argument. I'll think about it. I promise."

"Well, come to rehearsal with me."

"Not today. I'll let Mr. Car Tunes get settled in first, then . . . maybe."

TJ stood up when I did and gave me a really big hug. "Thanks, Mango."

As I hurried away, I couldn't stop thinking about what he said earlier. He said he *loved* me. He actually, really said it. Did he mean it? I mean, like, did he mean LOVE like IN LOVE, or love like "love ya bro" kind of love? OMGZ, this was all so confusing. I couldn't wait to talk to Izzy and see what she thought.

Mango in the City

On my way into the building, I saw a big black SUV with tinted windows idling by the curb. I guess I noticed it because it looked kind of menacing. I was staring so hard, I wasn't watching where I was going and I bumped into a guy in a chauffeur uniform coming around the front of the car. Zippy's coffee went flying through the air and smashed against the car's window. I froze, a deer in headlights. The window slid down, and that's when I got my first glimpse of him.

Gabriel Faust!

CHAPTER FIFTEEN

The Ego Has Landed

The chauffeur didn't apologize for sending the coffee flying out of my hand. Okay, so I kind of bumped into him too, but still, he could have said something. Rude! I guess he was too busy to talk to me—he had to open the back door of the SUV.

As Gabriel Faust stepped out of the SUV, wearing oversize sunglasses that covered most of his face, everything went music video magical. Gabriel Faust's biggest hit, "Rainbows, Lollipops, Gumdrops & You," began playing in my head. It was like he was moving in slow motion. When his feet touched the sidewalk, I realized he wasn't as tall as he seemed on television, but his hair, those golden locks, cascaded around his angelic face just the way they did in his music videos. A few girls who happened to be walking by screamed when they recognized him and tried to follow him into the building. The rude chauffeur held his arms out to keep them away, and *whoosh*—Gabriel Faust was gone. Music video magic over.

Still stunned, I rebooted and began walking, zombie-like,

into the building. Suddenly, Gabriel Faust wasn't merely a two-dimensional pop star on the inside of my closet door that I used to practice kissing. He was a real, flesh and blood and golden locks human being, and he had just brushed past me as he went by, trailing stardust.

Although I could've gotten into the same elevator as Gabriel Faust, I didn't. I waited for the next one. I thought about getting in with him and introducing myself, but I was too . . . what? Starstruck? Thunderstruck? Too struck with something to assert myself. And anyway, the rude chauffeur probably would have blocked me from entering, so it was better to wait.

When I got to the sixteenth floor, a thought occurred to me. I didn't want to meet Gabriel Faust looking nine or ten years old! I ran to the ladies' room. There were some dancers and actresses that must have been from other shows at the sinks, washing their hands or checking their hair in the mirror. I stepped into a stall. I wasn't experienced putting on makeup, and I certainly didn't want them watching me doing it.

Sitting on the toilet, I took my cell phone and the pink lipstick out of my backpack. Then I opened my camera app and used it as a mirror as I applied the lipstick. I did it slowly, making sure I didn't smear it like a clown, the way I did when I first got into my mother's makeup when I was four years old. To this day, she still cracks up her friends telling them how shocked she had been when I crept up behind her, "looking like Boo-Boo the clown!" I rubbed my lips together, checked myself out in the camera, and my lipstick application was perfect. Maybe no one else would notice I was wearing it, but I knew and when I got up, I felt I was standing a little bit straighter and taller. How could I have known that tall was the last thing I should have been trying to be today?

When I entered the rehearsal studio, everyone was crowded around Gabriel Faust. They were clapping and taking selfies and generally fawning—especially Zippy. Now, this was odd, because just yesterday she had gone on and on about how much of a has-been Gabriel Faust was, how he couldn't really sing, blah, blah, blah. But now, it was as though her pupils had been replaced by the Klieg lights used to sweep across the sky at movie premieres, and she was beaming five hundred watts worth of baloney. Interesting. I was beginning to think Zippy's DNA was missing a sincerity chromosome.

In the midst of all this adoration, Gabriel Faust was stone-faced. There wasn't even a hint of a smile. It was as though he were a mannequin in a wax museum. None of the excitement he was causing seemed to be affecting him in the least. I was starting to feel a mango pit growing in my stomach, the same one I got when I was nervous or afraid or completely insecure.

Bob clapped his hands together and used his booming voice to calm everybody down and proceed with the rehearsal. He thanked Gabriel Faust for joining the company. He introduced himself and Larry and then he scanned the room until his eyes found me. "Oh, there she is, your co-star. Mango, come on over here."

All eyes were on me as I walked across the studio toward *him*. I was torn between feeling like a star walking down the red carpet at a movie premiere and Joan of Arc on my way to being burned at the stake. But the most overwhelming thought running through my head was the realization that I should have actually *used* the bathroom before entering the rehearsal studio. OMGZ, it was not easy to walk across a room while trying to hold your legs together and keep your bladder in check at the same time.

Finally, I was standing in front of Gabriel Faust. "Hi," I squeaked.

Gabriel Faust removed his oversize sunglasses, looked up at me, cranked out a forced smile, and mumbled, "Wow, she's tall."

Uh-oh . . .

He beckoned the rude chauffeur and whispered in his ear. The chauffeur nodded and hurried out of the room, and Gabriel Faust turned away from me as though I had vanished. Bob and Larry proceeded to introduce the rest of the cast as if nothing had happened, but I noticed Bob shoot a worried glance my way. I was left standing there, holding my long legs together and wondering if I was going to be fired.

I was so glad when the intros were done and Acorn called out, "Take five! We'll start the read-through when we're back in."

Yes! A chance to escape back to the ladies' room and talk myself down from my gloomy self-conscious cloud. It wasn't my fault I was tall, just like it wasn't Gabriel Faust's fault that he was, well, shorter than me. I mean, he looked way taller on TV. Maybe there was a way for him to look taller onstage, too. Or could I look shorter? I bent my knees a little bit as I hurried to the restroom. No, that felt weird. Anywho, that wasn't my problem to worry about. I couldn't help my height. All I could do was concentrate on being the best Juliet I could be.

On my way back from the restroom, I passed what seemed like a heated discussion between Bob, Larry and a lady I had never seen before. From her body movements, she seemed powerful and confident to the extreme. She was an African American woman about the same complexion as my mom, curvy to the max, really tall, and wearing a lot of makeup and a bush of pink hair that was styled to look like a chrysanthemum! I almost couldn't stop staring at her, but then I remembered what that had led to earlier . . . As I passed the intense trio, the powerful lady held her huge hand out in a "stop" gesture and said, "Your needs are not my concern, gentlemen. I'm here to advocate for my client, and that's that."

I tried to linger by the door to hear more, but as soon as I entered the room, Zippy hustled over to me. "Hey, kiddo, where's my coffee?"

Oops! "Uh, well, I had a little accident on the way into the building. See, it was knocked out of my hand and—"

"Oh! You're the one who baptized Gabe's ride!"

"You know about that?"

"Word travels fast, clumsy." She laughed. "Talk about getting started on the wrong foot. Well, maybe he's the forgiving type. I doubt it, but there's always hope, I guess." She cocked her head to the side with a *yeah right* smirk and charged across the room to whisper to a group of chorus members.

Then Roz came up to me, real close. Flipping her long braids behind her shoulder, she said, "Mango, my child. Is that lipstick you're wearing today?"

"Yes."

"Your mother lets her twelve-year-old daughter wear makeup?"

To avoid answering her question with a lie, I said, "Twelve and a half."

Roz reached up and touched my Afro puff. "Mm, you have some nice thick hair. You ought to let me braid it for you. Give you some nice pigtails."

Her smile broadened as she turned and walked off. What was with this woman? Why was she obsessed with making me look young so she wouldn't look old?

Bob, Larry, and the powerful lady came into the room. Bob had Acorn gather the company, and then he made an announcement. "Okay, everyone except Mango is excused for the rest of the day. Be sure to take your scripts with you and spend the extra time getting familiar with your lines and the songs. I promise we'll have a full company rehearsal soon . . . hopefully tomorrow."

Zippy rushed up to Bob. "Do I have to stick around to take Mango home?"

"Don't worry about it," Bob said. "I'll see that she gets home safe."

"Okay, as long as I still get paid." Zippy shrugged and walked off. I didn't know she was getting paid to be my escort, but I guess it made sense. Why else would she go out of her way every day? It wasn't like we were friends or anything. As a matter of fact, it was very *unlikely* that we'd ever become friends at all. Maybe once I got used to being in the city, I could travel back and forth on my own. I doubted Mom and Dada would allow that, but . . . you never knew.

"All right, company. Let's all clear the space as quickly as possible," Acorn called out. "I'll text your call times later this afternoon."

There was a lot of chatter as the cast packed their gear and headed out. I noticed Gabriel Faust wasn't anywhere around. Was he excused for the rest of the day, too? Why was I the only one being held back? Uh-oh! Didn't they bring TJ in all by himself yesterday when they told him he was being replaced? Was the same thing about to happen to me?

Bob called me over to the table. "Mango Delight Fuller, I'd like to introduce you to—"

The powerful lady cut Bob off, jutted her Incredible Hulk hand toward me, and said, "Frances Francisco. Happy to meet you. I've heard so much about you. I'm Gabriel's manager. I've been representing him since his amazing talents revealed themselves when he was in first grade. I'm what you call a star-maker, star-promoter, and star-protector."

My hand was dwarfed in hers as we shook. "Nice to meet you," I said.

She held onto my hand and moved in closer. "I'm curious to see if you live up to the hype these two have built up around you. Piece of advice: lose the 'Fuller.' Mango Delight is the kind of name people won't forget, and since it's your real name, that makes it all the better." Her phone buzzed and she answered it by tapping the headset in her ear. "Yes? Right. We're ready now. Bring him up." She turned back to Bob, Larry, and me. "Excuse me, I've got couple of urgent calls to make." She gave an icy smile that was all teeth and very little warmth and walked to the other side of the room while commanding her phone to dial a number.

I looked at Bob and Larry, confused. "I know this is kind of weird . . ." Bob started.

"Kind of?" Larry said, rolling his eyes.

"Keep your cool, Larry, please." Bob turned back to me. "It seems Gabriel Faust is a little shy and his manager has requested a private read-through before we include the rest of the cast."

I gulped. "So, I'm not getting fired?" Across the room, Frances Francisco let out a whooping laugh that seemed to rattle all the mirrors in the space.

Bob put a hand on my shoulder. "Fired? Of course not. You're our Juliet."

Larry said, "You are here to stay, no matter what our Romeo and his big-haired minion have to say about it."

Bob elbowed him. "Cool it, Larry. She's probably got the hearing of a bat."

The door to the studio opened, and the rude chauffeur entered, looked around the room, then turned back and gave an all-clear signal. Gabriel Faust entered, walked directly across the room, and stood in front of me. As if by magic, he was suddenly about two inches taller and I had to look up at *him*. He nodded, turned to the rude chauffeur, and gave him a thumbs up.

I looked down and saw that Gabriel Faust was now wearing a pair of boots with heels and a thick platform that added inches to his height. So that was how they did it in Hollywood!

Gabriel took off his oversize sunglasses and headed for the table that had been set up with scripts and bottles of water. As soon as he took his seat, Frances Francisco was at his side. "Let's get started," she barked. "Gabriel has a recording studio booked until midnight, and we can't waste a minute."

Although this was only my second time doing a play, I was certain this would be the strangest, most uncomfortable read-through of my life, and I couldn't wait for it to be over. I was asked to sit directly across from Gabriel Faust. Bob, Mr. Ramsey, Acorn, and Frances Francisco all took seats, and we started the read-through. Acorn read the stage directions, I read Juliet, Gabriel Faust read Romeo, and Bob read all the other parts. Mr. Ramsey, at the piano, played and sang all the songs except mine, which I had to stand and do all alone.

I surprised myself by how comfortable I was singing in front of Gabriel Faust and his manager. It had been a while since I sang all my solos, but it felt really good, like putting on a favorite coat and finding a dollar I'd forgotten about in the pocket. Gabriel Faust kept his eyes on his script while I sang, but Frances Francisco, who had barely looked up from her phone during the entire read-through, actually glanced up and smiled at me once. I closed my eyes and as I sang, I let the music lift me high above my worries about working with a star who was nothing like I thought he'd be, and being far from home in New York City.

CHAPTER SIXTEEN

Attack of the 50-Foot Prima!

After rehearsal, Bob called a car service and had Acorn escort me back to Aunt Zendaya's. For the first five minutes of the ride, Acorn was busy on his phone texting call times to the cast and crew. Then, he undid his blonde man bun, shook his shoulder-length hair loose, and smiled at me. "So, how are you doing, Mango?"

"Um, fine, I guess. I'm not sure."

He chuckled. "Since you're not sure, I'll take a guess. Is that okay with you?"

I shrugged.

He pulled his legs onto the seat criss-cross applesauce style, ran his fingers through his hair, and looked at me very closely. "Let's see. I have a feeling you are confused and a bit overwhelmed. Being in New York, starring in a play with a famous person, being surrounded by so many adults all day, all of these new things have your head spooling up and down like a yo-yo."

"Yeah, that's it. I feel like a yo-yo spinning up, down, and all around. It's like someone is doing yo-yo tricks, and I don't know what's going to happen next."

"Yes. That's good. Just what you should be feeling."

"No, it's not good! I miss my family. I miss my friends, and my real life. I'm uncomfortable all the time."

Acorn leaned closer to me. "Mango, this *is* your real life. You've just stepped out of your comfort zone, and everything around you is new and happening very fast. But that just means one very important thing."

"What's that?"

"You're growing. Growth is never comfortable at first. Like stretching, it can really hurt at first, but the more you do it, the easier it becomes."

I thought about that for a minute. "I remember when I first started Girls On Track at school, I used to hate stretching before we ran," I said. "It was torture. But after a while, stretching started to feel good before and after practice."

"Exactly. That's what I'm saying. It's going to be the same with what you're doing now. Stick with it. Embrace that fact that things are going to be uncomfortable for a while, but one day soon, things will start falling into place and you'll start to fit in . . . until the next time you step out of your comfort zone."

I smiled. "Maybe after this, I'll just stick closer to home in my own comfort zone."

"No, you won't do that. You're talented. You have the soul of an artist, Mango. You won't thrive by staying in comfort."

"How do you know?"

"Tell me, when they offered you the chance to come to New York and star in *Yo, Romeo!,* did you say no? Were you forced to come?"

"No. I wanted to come. No one forced me."

"Exactly. Your instincts pushed you out of your comfort zone before you even realized it. And now here you are, stretching and growing and learning new things. By the time these six weeks are over, you won't be the same Mango you were when we started. You'll be a different Mango"

I giggled. "I hope you're right."

"Oh, I'm right. Trust. I'm a very intuitive person."

"What does that mean?"

"It means I'm very good at sensing and understanding what people are feeling. It's a gift."

"Do you understand what Gabriel Faust is feeling? Because I sure don't."

Acorn tilted his head and took a deep breath. "I think he is very afraid and confused right now. That's why he hides behind those huge sunglasses. He is worried that he may not or cannot be what people expect him to be. That is common for famous people, but it is even more intense for Gabriel Faust because he is so young and has been famous for so long, perhaps too long."

"That's sad."

"In a way it is. Just like you, he is stepping out of his comfort zone, except he is afraid that if he fails, he will be letting millions of his fans down. You're both in the same boat. If you want to grow, Mango, it's up to you to pick up the oars and row to shore or sit still, spring a leak, and eventually sink."

I leaned back on the seat and looked at Acorn. He was so calm and so easy to talk to. I wished he was the one escorting me to and from rehearsals every day. I asked, "Is Acorn your real name?"

"It is the name I was given when I had no choice, so yes. What about you? Is Mango Delight Fuller your real name or a stage name?"

"It's the name I was given when I had no choice."

He nodded. "Names are very important. I have a sister named Maple Leaf and a brother named Branch. I am Acorn. I start small but grow into a big tree." He smiled at me. "You are Mango, a fruit that will ripen to the ultimate sweetness."

When we got to Aunt Zendaya's building, Acorn escorted me all the way up the four flights. Aunt Zendaya was busy making jewelry when we entered the apartment, but she stopped what she was doing as soon as she saw Acorn and came across the room to greet him.

I made the introductions. "Aunt Zendaya, this is Acorn. Acorn, this is my aunt."

Acorn held out his hand. "Pleased to meet you."

Aunt Zendaya smiled. "Likewise. What is your role with the production?"

"He's the stage manager," I said. "He's in charge of

scheduling and telling us when to take breaks and making sure everything is ready for rehearsal."

"That's correct." Acorn said. "And once rehearsals are done and the director leaves, I run the show.

Aunt Zendaya invited Acorn to stay for dinner. I gulped when he said yes, a little worried he was going to have to endure a practically flavorless meal. Acorn followed Aunt Z into her tiny kitchen, and I settled in on the futon to text TJ.

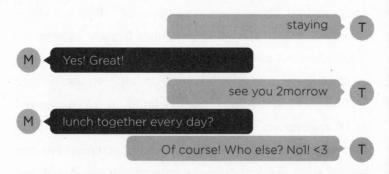

M Going or staying? What's the what?

The little dots started pulsing right away. A good sign, I hoped?

staying T

M Yes! Great!

see you 2morrow T

M lunch together every day?

Of course! Who else? No1! <3 T

Yes! I was beyond happy. I immediately face2faced Izzy and filled her in on everything that had happened today. She wasn't as excited as I thought she'd be when I told her about meeting Gabriel Faust. I began to wonder if maybe our friendship wasn't back on track the way I'd hoped it would be. "Is everything okay?" I asked.

"Yeah and no," she said.

"What does that mean?"

"Well, you father and Jasper came by this afternoon."

Oh, man, I'd completely forgotten to ask her about that! I'd been so caught up in my own things that I hadn't thought to check in on what was going on with her. I felt like a self-centered jerk. "How did it go?" I asked

"Well, it started out great. Jasper was so happy to see me, until mi prima, Carmella, came into the room."

"Your cousin? When did she arrive?"

"Late last night. OMGZ, she is the most overbearing, self-centered egomaniac that I've ever known! I don't remember her being this way when we were kids."

"How long has it been since you've seen her?"

"About six or seven years? And when she leaves, I'll make sure it's twenty years before I see her again! Do you know what happened today with Jasper?"

"No. And I won't know until you tell me!"

"Well," Izzy said with a big sigh. "I was hugging Jasper, and Carmella comes up and snatches him from me and starts hugging him and pinching his cheeks and tickling him. When I took him back, he started crying and reaching his arms to go back to Carmella!"

"No!"

"Yes! It was like *Invasion of the Body Snatchers* or something! I think he thought she was me."

"How? That's not possible."

"Well, maybe it is. I guess she kinda sorta looks like me and sounds like me and *ugh*! She is just so—" Suddenly, Izzy stopped herself. She put a bright smile on her face and said, "Carmella! Hey, girl, what are you up to?"

I heard another voice from off-screen. "Nothing. Nothing at all. Who are you talking to?"

Suddenly, a new face appeared on my phone right next to Izzy. I almost did a double take because they looked like they were twins! Same face, same size as far as I could tell, but Carmella was like Izzy 2.0. It was like they were the same picture, but Carmella had double the pixels.

Carmella took Izzy's phone and started talking to me like Izzy wasn't even there. "Oh, you must be Mango! Izzy told me so much about you. I hear you're starring in a show on Broadway."

"Well . . . it's actually way, way off Broadway."

"Well, you're way-way closer to Broadway than Izzy, that's for sure. Oh, I met your little hermano, Jasper, today. We fell instantly in love with each other. And your father baked such amazing blueberry scones!" She placed a hand over her heart. "Oh! I was amazed by how good they tasted. I forgot all about my allergy to carbs and how I was gonna watch my figure while I'm here this summer. I am not going to let Izzy make me fat!" She laughed loud and long, and I smiled, trying to be polite, wondering what happened to Izzy.

"Uh, where'd Izzy go?"

"Oh, she's right here looking like a grumpy face. So tell me, how is the play going?"

I didn't want to be rude, so I was stuck face2facing with Carmella for another ten minutes until she announced she was going to the bathroom. "Here, Izzy, hold the phone. I'll be right back, Mango!"

Izzy looked downright miserable when she reappeared on the screen. "See what I mean? Now she's stealing my best friend. She's unbearable. And she's going to be here for the rest of the summer unless I can arrange an alien abduction."

"Izzy, I think she's just trying to be nice."

"Yeah, nice like a bulldozer."

"I'm sorry you're not having fun, Izzy. Maybe if you give it some time you two will connect again?"

"I'd rather swallow golf balls spiked with nails. Uh-oh, here she comes! I gotta get off before she hijacks my phone again. Talk to you later. Bye!"

Just like that, she hung up. I wasn't sure what I'd say to her anyway. I had never seen Izzy like this before. She was always so bubbly and confident and outspoken. Now she was the opposite of her usual self in every way. It was as though Carmella had stolen her personality.

I heard laughter coming from the kitchen along with the sounds of pans sizzling. The most surprising thing was the aroma. Aunt Z's little studio apartment was filled with smells of something good to eat. My stomach growled, and I realized I had hardly eaten anything the whole day.

Aunt Zendaya floated out of the kitchen and set three plates and utensils on the coffee/dining table. "Mango, why didn't you tell me your stage manager was a master chef?"

"I didn't know?"

"Well, he is!" She leaned in, eyes sparkling, and whispered, "And he's awfully cute, too."

She glided back into the kitchen, and I listened as her laughter filled the air in a really jolly way, like sleigh bells. It reminded me of the way Mom sounded whenever she and Dada were flirting. And then I thought . . . uh-oh.

CHAPTER SEVENTEEN

The Magic Bubble

A corn had to be the best chef in the world next to Dada, or maybe he was the best vegan chef in the world. Dinner was great—the flavors, textures, and colors of the food were amazing. Aunt Zendaya was begging him to give her cooking lessons. Secretly, I was begging him, too! The two of them got along really well, and there was a point when they were so deep in conversation, I'm pretty sure they forgot I was there. After Acorn left, around 11, Aunt Zendaya wouldn't stop asking me all sorts of questions about him, but I couldn't tell her much because I'd only met him two days before and also I was exhausted and wanted to go to sleep!

When Zippy arrived the next morning to take me to rehearsal, Aunt Zendaya, who usually slept until at least eleven in the morning, suddenly needed to go to the market so she came downstairs with me. As we walked to the subway, Aunt Zendaya started peppering Zippy with questions about Acorn. I didn't know why I felt funny about it. I mean, Aunt Zendaya was a beautiful woman and single, as far as I knew.

She was trying to keep her questions about Acorn casual, but I could see Zippy's antennae of suspicion pop up when Aunt Zendaya asked, "How old do you think he is?"

Zippy raised an eyebrow. "I don't *think*. I know. He's twenty-two."

Aunt Zendaya was quiet for a moment, then said, "He's obviously very mature for his age."

Zippy threw me a *what's on her mind* glance, and I looked away. If Aunt Zendaya started dating Acorn, would that be weird? It would mean he would come over and cook more and maybe Aunt Zendaya's cooking would improve. But my mom was thirty-six, which meant Aunt Zendaya was thirty, a whole eight years older than Acorn. The odd thing is, that wouldn't make much difference if she were the man in the relationship. Many men marry women that are ten or even twenty years younger than they are. So, I decided, if Aunt Zendaya and Acorn started dating, I'd be fine with it. If they got married and had a baby, I'd be the one who brought them together! But hold on—they'd only cooked one meal together and here I was fantasizing about the rest of their lives. I needed to slow down! I had enough to think about without charting my aunt's future happiness.

I decided I was going to listen to Acorn's advice, grab ahold of my oars, and row my boat through the river of discomfort until I found my way back to comfortable shores again. My first obstacle: doing whatever I could to break, melt, or crush the ice with Gabriel Faust.

TJ was already in the rehearsal studio when I arrived. I was so happy to see him. "You're here!" I said. "So you're staying? You're going to understudy Romeo, right?"

"Yeah, you convinced me. I'll understudy Romeo and be in the chorus, too. Maybe even learn to dance."

"That's so great!" I threw my arms open wide and gave TJ a big hug. And in the moment, just that fraction of a second when we touched, I remembered him saying, *I love you* and that kiss after the party. Suddenly I started feeling weird. Not bad weird, but more like, *awk*-weird, because now I wasn't sure what I really meant by hugging him. So I sort of backed away quickly and changed the subject. "Lunch today? New York pizza?"

""Yep. Now until forever."

I decided to let TJ in on my master plan. "I'm going to make friends with Gabriel Faust today. Whatever I have to do to make him open up to me, I'm going to do it."

"Cool," TJ said, "I bet he's a nice guy underneath those humongous sunglasses."

I detected a drop of sarcasm in his comment but decided to let it slide. Operation Make Friends with a Star was in effect. No one knew better than I did that it took time and care to make a real friendship. I didn't want to come on too strong—especially if Acorn's intuition was right and Gabriel Faust was shy and afraid of stepping out of his comfort zone.

What happened next was so totally unexpected that I kind of felt like I'd been hit by a truck. Gabriel Faust came into the studio, took off his huge sunglasses, and looked around the room. Before I had a chance to walk over to him, he called out, "Mango! Hey!" and came charging across the room to wrap me up in a big hug.

Uh . . . what? This was not the guy I'd met the day before. He was like completely the opposite of the quiet, stone-faced mannequin from yesterday. This Gabriel Faust was warm and uber friendly and just like, well, Romper, the character he played on *Brat House*.

He took my hand and led me over to the table where we'd be having the read-through. "Come on, you sit next to me. Okay?"

"Sure. Yeah," I said, amazed that my plan was working even though I hadn't even had a chance to do anything.

"You're having lunch with me today, so we can get to know each other and everything."

"Oh. Yeah. That'd be great." I didn't know what was happening, but it seemed like everyone else in the room had disappeared and I was in a magic bubble. Just me and Gabriel Faust. He was all I could see, and my BCF was acting like all he could see was me.

The full cast read-through was a blur. I supposed I was saying my lines and singing my songs, but for all I knew, I could have just been sitting there saying, "Blah blah blahddy blah." I was still dazed when Acorn called the hour lunch break. As everyone was on their way out of the studio,

Mango in the City

I vaguely recalled TJ standing nearby waving to get my attention. The next thing I knew, the rude chauffeur was opening the back door to the big black SUV with the tinted windows and I was on my way to lunch with my second favorite star.

CHAPTER EIGHTEEN

Lunching in the Magic Bubble

The rude chauffeur turned out *not* to be rude after all. He asked me if I'd like a bottled water, told me to call him Josh, and then raised the tinted glass that separated the back of the SUV from the front. Immediately, Gabriel Faust started asking me a zillion questions.

"Where are you from? How old are you? How did you get started in the business? Who do you live with? How do you like New York? What else have you done? What kind of movies do you like? Do you like to read? Watch TV? Travel? Who's your favorite star?"

"Um . . . you and Beyoncé."

"Oh Bey, she's great. The best. So much fun to hang with."

"You know Beyoncé?"

"Yeah. Bey and Jay are like family, you know?"

I could NOT believe I was sitting next to someone who actually knew the queen of everything that mattered to me!

My heart started racing, but I didn't want to geek out in front of him, so I took a deep breath, counted to ten, and calmed myself before speaking again. "How did you meet them?"

"I think it was at the Grammys. I wasn't nominated, but I was presenting. It was a pain, but you know, something you just have to do in the biz. The after-parties are dope. They make it all worthwhile, you know?"

"No . . . not really. I've never been to an after-party. Actually, I've never even been to a *before* party."

"Well, stick with me and you'll get to go to lots of places you've never been before. You know what they say, right?"

"I don't think so . . ."

"Of course you do!" Gabriel Faust lifted his chin, widened his eyes, and cocked his head to the side just the way he used to do when he was a little kid on TV, and then he said it: "Brats rule, fools drool!"

I was stunned for a second, and then I thought I'd better laugh or clap or something. So I did both. I laughed and clapped and that seemed to make Gabriel Faust very happy as he took seated bows. "Works every time. Like magic!" he said.

About twenty minutes later, the SUV pulled up to the curb, and Josh hurried to open the door. I stepped out and looked around. We were on an almost deserted street, with a lot of old storefronts and warehouses, and none of them looked like a restaurant. Gabriel Faust stepped out after me, put on his huge sunglasses, and took my hand. "This way."

He led me to a dry cleaner. You know, where people take their clothes to get laundered. A bell above the door jingled as we walked in, and a woman with piercings in her ears, nose, and lips stepped out from behind a rack of clothes.

"Are we picking up your laundry?" I whispered.

Gabriel Faust lowered his head and looked at me over his huge sunglasses. "You're so funny. I love you!" Right away, I knew this wasn't *love* the way TJ had said it. This was more of a Hollywood-type, *love ya, babe"* kind of love.

"Right this way, Faustie," the hipster girl said, and she led us behind the counter and past the rack of clothes to a rusty metal door. She opened it, and my chin dropped so low, I thought it'd hit the floor.

Behind the door, hip-hop music was playing. The lights were low, and the walls were filled with abstract art and smoky mirrors. All around the room people were sitting at tables, eating. Gabriel was still holding my hand as the hipster girl led us across the room. I almost stumbled when we passed Will Smith. Yes, it was really him, the movie star, TV star, rapper—my mother would absolutely die if she knew I was this close to him! And at another table there was . . . no, it couldn't be, could it? OMGZ! I was positive it was Taylor Swift, rocking a pair of huge sunglasses even though the dark room was practically a cave!

We got seated at a fancy booth in a corner of the . . . I wasn't really sure what kind of place this was, so I asked.

Gabriel Faust laughed. "It's a restaurant, of course. One of my favorites. It's called The Cleaners."

I'd never heard of it. "Okay, but . . . was that Taylor—"

"Yeah, but try not to stare. Famous people come here to be around other famous people and just be themselves. No gawkers allowed, you know?"

I quickly turned my neck away from the rest of the room, but I really wanted to stare at T Swizzle and see if I could recognize any other famous faces.

"I'm one of the owners," Gabriel Faust told me.

"You are?"

"Yeah. I'm in an investment group, and my financial advisers take really good care of me and my money."

"That lady, Frances Francisco?"

"No, she's my manager. My personal pit bull. Nobody messes with me, because she is the czar of managers."

It was all so surreal. Me, Mango Delight Fuller, sitting across from a famous star in a room full of famous stars. All of a sudden, it was hard to catch my breath, and my hands began to shake.

"Hey, are you all right?" Gabriel Faust asked

"I don't know . . . I feel kind of dizzy."

He waved his hand and a waiter appeared, like magic. "Get some water, quick."

The waiter came back as fast as lighting with a glass and four bottles of water. "Flat or sparkling, cold or room temperature?"

I pointed to the room temperature, and he filled my glass.

As I sipped, I began to calm down a little bit. Gabriel Faust leaned forward. "Are you okay?" he asked again.

"Yes, I'm fine. I guess I just went a little mega-gaga for a moment. I mean, I've never been in a place like this with real stars and . . . I guess my brain needed a chance to catch up to my life and realize I'm sitting in a place like this about to have lunch with Gabriel Faust!"

"Faustie."

"Huh?"

"Faustie. My squad calls me Faustie."

"Faustie . . . okay, Faustie!"

"So, what would you like for lunch?"

"May I see a menu, please?"

"There are no menus here. You can order anything you want—sushi, pasta, salads, steak, chicken, smoothies, or even chicken smoothies. Anything your heart desires."

The thought of chicken smoothies didn't go down too well, but I did have another idea. "Since coming to New York, I've been living with my vegan aunt, and I keep dreaming about bacon cheeseburgers."

"Your wish is my command." He lifted his hand and the waiter magically reappeared. Gabriel—I mean, Faustie—ordered a bacon cheeseburger for me and then roast duck empanadas and soup dumplings for himself.

After the waiter left, I smiled at Faustie for a couple of awkward seconds. "You know," I said, "you're so different from yesterday."

He shrugged. "I guess I'm a little shy at first. It takes me a while to get in character around people I don't know. It's kind of weird when you're famous. People expect you to be a certain way and you really just want to be yourself, but at the same time, you're scared that if you are just being yourself, you'll disappoint your fans."

"I'm a fan, and I'm not disappointed."

"Thanks. But I also have to be careful. Show business is hard, and I've learned that you can't just trust everyone who is nice to you." He paused for a few seconds and scanned the room, then continued. "People in this business usually want something from you and will do just about anything to get it. You really have to be smart and careful about who to trust."

I knew what he meant. After being betrayed by my BFFN (best friend for never), Brooklyn, I was trying to be really careful about who I became friends with or let get close to me.

Our lunch came, and I took a bite out of the best bacon cheeseburger in the world. The burger was so juicy and flavorful, the bacon perfectly crisp, the cheese so warm and gooey. I couldn't help myself—I squealed after that first bite.

Faustie offered me one of his duck empanadas, but before I could take one, my phone started buzzing. I told Faustie I had to check my phone in case it was my parents, but it wasn't them. It was a face2face from Izzy. "Oh, it's just my friend. I'll call her back."

"No way! Answer it. Go ahead." Then a devilish smile spread across his face. "Better yet, let me answer it!"

OMGZ! I knew Izzy loved Gabriel Faust, but this might give her a heart attack. Then again, it would be so spicy, and this could be just the pick-me-up she needed. "Okay, go ahead," I said.

Faustie took my phone and answered it. "Hello! Mango's phone."

There was a pause and then I heard Izzy say, "Um, is Mango there?"

"Yes, she's here. We're having lunch."

"You are? But who are . . . wait a minute! OMGZ! Do you know who you are?"

Faustie laughed. "I'm pretty sure I do most of the time."

"You're Gabriel Faust!" Izzy screamed so loud that even through the phone, it made the people at nearby tables turn and stare.

I took the phone back from Faustie. "Izzy, calm down! Shhhh!"

Izzy covered her mouth. "Mango!" she stage-whispered. "You're having lunch with your all-time celebrity crush!"

That was embarrassing. I mean, yes, it was true, but did she have to say it out loud right in front of my *all-time celebrity crush*? "Izzy!"

"Okay, okay, okay! All right, I'm calm now. So calm. Calm as a clam. Can I speak to him again?"

"I thought you called to speak to me!"

"Let's be real, Mango. I can speak to you anytime, but Gabriel Faust, I mean, come on! Please!"

I looked to Faustie. He nodded and held his hand out for the phone. "Hi, Izzy," he said. "I'm Faustie. What do you want to talk to me about?"

There was a long pause before I heard Izzy again. "Um . . . I don't know. I just, I want to look at you for a minute and then tell you that I loved your show, even though I didn't have cable when it first came on, but I've seen all the episodes on YouTube, and I like your songs and I wish I could meet you in person."

"Well, maybe that can be arranged."

It can? I mean, maybe, that would be so uber crispy!"

"All right, I'll see what I can do. Nice meeting you, Izzy," Faustie said, and handed the phone back to me.

I giggled at how star-struck Izzy looked. "I have to finish lunch and get back to rehearsal," I told her. "I'll call you tonight."

"Girl, you'd better. If you don't, I'll summon the ghost of my Aunt Maria Magdalena and tell her to haunt you until you do. And believe me, you'll never sleep again when you see what she looks like after all these years being dead!"

In the background at Izzy's house, I heard, "Izzy, who are talking to?"

"Oh no!" Izzy said. "It's the body snatcher. Gotta go, bye!"

"Bye," I said, and hung up. I turned back to Faustie. "Sorry about that."

"Nothing to be sorry about. I like her. Maybe we can fly her up for opening night or something."

"Are you serious?"

"Of course I am. It's important to have your friends around to share your great moments with you. Keeps you grounded."

At that exact deliriously happy moment, just as I was about to take another bite of the greatest bacon cheeseburger ever, Faustie's eyes popped out and he did a double take worthy of the character he played on TV. He was staring at someone or something over my shoulder. Remembering what he'd said earlier, I didn't want to turn around and gawk, but from his expression, I knew it was someone super important. Maybe even Beyoncé! I couldn't help myself. I turned to look and then I saw her. The star of my favorite TV show, *Cupcakers,* and Faustie's ex-bae. It was her. In the flesh! Destiny Manaconda!

CHAPTER NINETEEN

Pop! Goes the Bubble

So there I was in between two of the biggest stars in my world. I was frozen, with my teeth inches away from a juicy bacon cheeseburger that was dripping down my palm. Everything Destiny Manaconda was wearing was on trend or beyond. Her bubblegum pink hair, perfect. Her makeup, perfect. Her nails, perfect! How could anyone be so perfect? She looked like she'd just stepped off the cover of *Vogue*.

Faustie stood and said, "Destiny, hey girl. What's good?"

Destiny glared at him. "Who told you I'd be here?"

"No one. What are you talking about? I was just having lunch with—"

As he held his hand out to introduce me, Destiny Manaconda flashed her amazing, heavily lashed hazel eyes at me. "Do you mind?" she said. "A little privacy. Thanks so much, sweetness."

With that, she lifted her hand and a waiter appeared out of nowhere, picked up my plate and water, and led me across the room to a booth. The bacon cheeseburger juice was now on my wrist as I slid into my seat about to pass out because I hadn't inhaled for about forty seconds.

When I finally did breathe, I looked across the room and saw Faustie and Destiny Manaconda seated across from each other, having a heated conversation. Their eyes were flashing angry darts back and forth. They were jabbing their fingers in the air accusingly at each other. Then Destiny Manaconda pointed her finger in my direction, and I quickly looked down. I put my perfect bacon cheeseburger back on the plate and used a linen napkin to wipe up the burger juice that had made its way past my wrist.

I didn't know what to do. I tried to act natural, as if nothing was going on, but I wasn't sure what to do with my hands and I bet I looked like a confused mannequin in a department store window.

Now Faustie and Destiny Manaconda were yelling at each other. It was the only sound in the whole restaurant, and it seemed as though everyone was looking from them to me and back again. I lifted my bacon cheeseburger and took a tiny bite, but my taste buds must've been traumatized because all the flavor was gone. It tasted dry and bitter, like ashes of humiliation. I couldn't just sit here like this. I had to do something! So I took out my phone and face2faced Izzy. She picked up immediately.

"Mango! Hi girl! What's going on?"

"I'm still at lunch with Gabriel Faust, and Destiny Manaconda just showed up!" I whisper-shouted.

146

"What? Gabriel Faust? You're eating lunch with my dream man?"

I was stumped for a second. Izzy would know who I was having lunch with. And then it came to me. "Carmella, is that you?"

"Of course, who did you think it was?"

"Well, this is Izzy's phone, so I thought I was talking to—"

In the background at Izzy's, I heard, "Carmella, give my phone!"

"In a minute, prima, I'm talking to Mango!"

"Mango is my friend, not yours!"

"Is too!"

"Is not!"

"Is too!"

I had had enough! With all the drama going on in the restaurant, the last thing I needed was more drama going on between Izzy and Carmella. "Cut it out!" I yelled. If it was even possible, the restaurant got ever quieter than it had been before. I looked up from my screen, and everyone was *definitely* looking at me. I looked down again and lowered my voice to a whisper. "Look, I can be friends with both of you, but I called to speak to Izzy. I'm in a crisis here, and I need to speak to Izzy now, so Carmella, please give her back her phone."

The phone changed hands and Izzy—the real Izzy—appeared on the screen. "Hold on," she said. She disappeared from the screen for a few seconds, and then she was back. "Okay, we can talk now."

Her voice sounded echoey, so I said, "Where are you?"

"I'm in the shower in the bathroom, the only place I can get some privacy these days. Okay, so what's the crisis?"

I whispered, "Destiny Manaconda is here."

Izzy shouted, "What? Shut up! Are you trying to give me a stroke? What?"

I nodded. "She just showed up out of the blue."

"Did you tell her how much you love her? How *Cupcakers* is your all-time favorite show?"

I shook my head, "I didn't get a chance. She ordered me to go away?"

"Ordered you? How dare she!"

"Now they're both at the table arguing."

Izzy gasped. "About their breakup?"

"I don't know, but she keeps pointing at me."

Izzy yelped, "Holy jealousy! She probably thinks he's dating you!"

"No way!"

"She walks into a restaurant and sees the two of you having an intimate rendezvous."

"It's no rendezvous, and there was nothing 'intimate' about it. We were just eating lunch."

"Were you holding hands? Were you gazing into each other's eyes? Did he have his arm around your shoulder?"

"No, no, and no!" Right then, Destiny Manaconda stood up from her table and started walking in my direction. I held up my phone to shield my face. "She's coming my way!"

Izzy said, "Duck! Get under the table! If you have to, use your phone as a weapon!"

I was almost on the verge of panic, but Destiny Manaconda walked right past my table without even glancing at me. Then Faustie went by, calling after her, "Destiny! Des, baby! Wait!" He didn't seem to notice me either. I sat back in my chair and let out a deep sigh of relief.

Izzy cried out, "What happened? What's going on?"

"They just left."

"The restaurant?"

"Yeah . . ."

"What are you gonna do now?"

"I don't know. Wait, I guess? We're supposed to be back at rehearsal soon, but I don't know where I am or how to get back."

Izzy started to say something, but her image froze and a "low battery" notification popped up on my screen. I was down to less than ten percent. In a couple of seconds, Izzy was gone. I tried calling her back, but it wouldn't go through.

I looked around the room. The hum of several conversations had returned, along with the scraping of silverware and the tinkling of ice in glasses. My bacon cheeseburger had deflated, which was okay because I didn't have an appetite anymore anyway. The minutes ticked by slowly. Taylor Swift and her entourage passed by my table as they made their way toward the exit. A waiter with movie star looks approached and placed a leather thingy that holds the check you're supposed to pay in front of me, saying, "Whenever you're ready, Miss."

No way! Did they really expect me to pay the bill? On my twenty dollar a day allowance? There was no way I could pay for a perfect bacon cheeseburger and duck whatchamacallums! Even so, I reached toward the leather thingy and opened it. The bill came to two hundred dollars and . . . my eyes became too tear-filled to comprehend the rest of the numbers.

As I moved to close the leather thingy, Josh, the chauffeur, appeared. "Ready to go?" he asked.

"Yes, but . . ."

"Don't worry, it's all taken care of."

"Um . . . Faustie? I mean Gabriel Faust, is he in the car?"

"No, sorry. He left in Miss Manaconda's car."

"Oh . . ."

I was in a stupor as we left, and I don't think I could feel my feet as Josh guided me to the SUV and drove back to rehearsal.

─

I was forty-five minutes late when I stepped onto the elevator to get to the sixteenth floor. Just as the doors were about to close, Frances Francisco slid in. She held a dill-pickle-size finger to her lips until the doors were completely shut and we were alone. Then she leaned in. "The gag is, Gabriel got sick and had to be rushed to his private physician. Got it?"

I didn't know what to say, so I just stared at her. She leaned in closer and snapped her dill pickle fingers in my face and repeated, "Got it? That's what you tell the producers, the press, your mama, and anyone else who comes nosing around. Capiche?"

I nodded.

"Good girl." She patted me on the back with her baseball mitt hand. The elevator doors slid open, and she ushered me into the rehearsal room.

Cartier, the choreographer, was teaching the company a dance routine to one of my solos, and the room smelled of sweat. Bob and Larry, going over the script at their table, looked up at me with disappointment clouding their eyes.

Frances Francisco went over to them and spilled "the gag," the lie I was supposed to tell anyone who asked. The truth of how and why I had been left behind was humiliating enough, and now I was being was ordered to lie about it, too. I didn't really know why, but I felt ashamed. Was I so unimportant to Gabriel Faust that he could leave me behind without a thought? Did he take me to that restaurant just to make Destiny Manaconda jealous? The first thing out of her mouth was, "Who told you I'd be here?" So yeah, maybe he did use me . . .

I felt like such a dope. Gabriel Faust himself had warned me about show business and how people were out to use you. He warned me and then made an example of me. As much as I wanted to, as much as my chest ached to let it all out,

I couldn't just stand there and cry like a baby. It was time for Mango Delight Fuller to grow a thick skin. I joined the company in front of the mirror, tried my best to focus on Cartier through wet eyes, and learned the dance.

One, two, three, turn left, turn right, hitch kick, step, repeat. One, two, three, turn left, turn right, hitch kick, step, repeat.

I watched my reflection in the mirror. The higher I kicked, the faster I turned, the thicker my skin.

CHAPTER TWENTY

Liar, Liar!

D etermination is an amazing thing. I was determined not to cry. Not to let my feelings show. Not to let on to anyone that I had been humiliated. My determination made me focus on choreography like never before. I was so focused, I forgot that I was the kind of dancer who usually looked like she was dancing to the beat of a song that hadn't played yet. Not only did I get all the steps down, but I was able to dance while singing my song, too! Without getting winded!

As rehearsal was ending, Cartier came up to me. "Mango, you were amazing. I mean, I thought I was going to have to work with you one-on-one to get you up to speed, but you killed it. You even learned faster than some of the professional dancers."

"Thanks."

"And you're not even breathing hard. What gives? Are you some kind of athlete?"

"No . . . I mean, I was on the track team at school."

"Oh, that's it. Runners build up breath control and stamina. Good for you! See you tomorrow."

Yes! Pride smashed humiliation! I was feeling good again. Even though I knew my muscles would be tighter than ever by tomorrow, right now I was feeling great. I looked around to find TJ and saw him heading out with a few of the other cast members around our age. I called, "TJ!"

He looked around, waved and stopped where he was. I walked up to him, "That was kind of fun, huh?"

"Yeah, it was cool." He said this looking over his shoulder at the cast members heading out to the hall.

I tried to refocus his attention on me. "Um. Cartier is a great choreographer."

"Sure is. Look, I'm gonna ride uptown with these guys . . ."

"Okay. Sure."

"We started hanging out when they took pity on me having lunch by myself. You know, at the pizzeria where we were supposed to go today?"

"Oh. Yeah . . . that's right. Sorry, TJ. Faustie—"

"Faustie? Whoa. That was lightning speed. You guys getting along real good, huh?"

"Actually—'"

Someone from the hall yelled, "Hey, Teej, elevator's here!"

TJ turned toward them, "Coming!" Then back to me, "Gotta go. Later."

He turned and jogged out of the room just like that. Dang.

How did I forget that we had planned to have lunch together? It was my idea, and I didn't even think of him when Faustie invited me to lunch. Maybe I should have asked if TJ could come along? I was a little surprised that TJ was so touchy about it. I mean, I told him about my plan to break the ice with Faustie. He should have understood why I had to go. Shouldn't he?

Zippy came up to me, her curly hair plastered to her head like she'd just come out of the shower. "Oof! That Cartier was out for blood today. Does she really expect us to do like backflips and sing at the same time?"

"We're not doing backflips."

"It's just an expression, kiddo."

"Oh . . . I think the dance is cool. Fun."

Zippy's lip curled into a snarl and she rolled her eyes. "Of course you would. I heard her over there telling you how phenomenal you were."

"She didn't say 'phenomenal.'"

"Whatever, kiddo." She pulled a towel from her backpack and ruffled it through her hair. "Just because she's blowing smoke up your butt doesn't mean you have to inhale. She's trying to buddy up with you 'cause you're the star. They all do that."

"They all who?"

"Anybody in the industry who's on the come up. This gig is a stepping stone for her. If she gets in good with you and you become a star, then she'll have an in."

"What do you mean?"

"She thinks you'll request her to choreograph all your shows if you hit it big. Believe me, be careful not to let your head get too big too fast." She grabbed her backpack and headed for the door. "I'm gonna stop in the ladies'. Meet you at the elevator."

As I went to gather my stuff, I glanced over to where Acorn was. He looked like he was busy going over something with Bob and Larry and one of the producers. I wished he were taking me back to Aunt Zendaya's instead of Zippy. I bet Aunt Zendaya hoped so, too. Oh well . . . I grabbed my stuff and headed for the elevator.

Zippy and I didn't talk on our way out of the building or walking to the subway. She didn't duck and dive through the oncoming people the way she had this morning. I guess the afternoon of choreography had slowed her down a bit.

On the platform waiting for the train, she was busy looking at her phone. So I looked at the people all around me. There were so many, heading home from work or wherever. I started trying to figure out what kind of jobs they had based on the clothes they were wearing. There was a guy with lavender hair wearing an orange tie-dyed T-shirt and fashionably ripped jeans—definitely some kind of artist. A short lady in a sharp, fitted business suit wearing sneakers was probably some big executive's assistant on her way to becoming the big boss someday.

Zippy tapped me on the shoulder. "So what really happened to Gabe today, huh? Did he really get sick?"

"Ummm . . ." I flashed back to Frances Francisco looming over me in the elevator and warning me not to tell even my mama the truth. I cleared my throat. I hated lying. I didn't want to actually say yes, so I kind of hummed, "Mm-hmm."

Zippy said, "So, was he or wasn't he sick?"

"That's what his manager said."

"I know what *she* said. They always cover up for their little spoiled has-beens. You were there. Tell me what really happened."

I bit my lip. My fingernails started brushing up against my thumb, and I wanted to gnaw on them so badly. A debate started in my head: Why should I keep Faustie's secret after he ghosted me? But if I told the truth, he might hate me. Even worse, I'd be on Frances Francisco's bad side, and that would be a horrible place to be. Finally I said, "He got sick and rushed off to his doctor. His stomach or something. I think it might have been something he ate?"

Zippy looked at me, eyes narrowing and her round face getting redder and redder by the second. "You're lying to me."

"I'm not!"

"You're a liar, that's what you are. Look!" She held up her phone and showed me a post on Gabby Glamour's gossip site. There were several paparazzi shots of Gabriel Faust and Destiny Manaconda in a park, holding hands and hugging.

The headline read, "Fausta-Conda Back 2gether Again for the 3rd Time."

My cheeks flared hotter than a blow torch. I just stood there with my mouth open, trying to get some words out, trying to explain that I was told to tell that story, but I just sputtered air.

Zippy snapped her cell phone case closed. "You know what, kiddo? I don't have time for liars and prima donnas who think they can take two-hour lunch breaks, come in, and show off their dancing and singing to make the rest of us look bad. No. Uh-uh! Tell you what, you can get someone else to take you to and from rehearsal. It's not worth the measly fifty dollars a week to hang around with a habitual liar."

Just then, hot air whooshed onto the platform as a train rushed into the station and screeched to a halt. The doors opened, and a flood of people spilled out of the train while other people pushed to get in. I got caught up in the middle of the anxious transfer and found myself inside the subway car, crushed against a pole. The ear assaulting announcement over the speaker said, "This is the number 5 Express to Flatbush Avenue. Watch the closing doors."

I turned to make sure Zippy was with me, and there she was, still on the platform with a fiendishly gleeful smirk on her face. She wiggled her fingers as the doors slid closed, and then the train lurched and took off into the blackness of the tunnel.

CHAPTER TWENTY-ONE

Abandoned

As the train rumbled through the tunnel, the lights flickered off and on several times. I held on tightly to the pole. My heart was racing. I was scared and on the verge of panic. I was confused, but most of all, I was angry. I couldn't believe the look on Zippy's face. That smirk and the way she wiggled her stubby little fingers as the train pulled off. She had stayed on the platform on purpose!

Some people cried when they got angry. I usually did. The thing was, at this moment, I was beyond anger—I was furious. I was NOT going to let Zippy bring me to my knees. People had tried it before. Like when Brooklyn signed me up to audition for *Yo, Romeo!* hoping I would melt into a puddle of humiliation. I showed her. Now here I was in New York City on my own—I was not going to cry.

I knew that our regular subway stop was Bergen Street, so I just had to stay on the train until then and walk the few blocks back to Aunt Zendaya's apartment building. No problem. Zippy said she wasn't going to be my escort anymore.

Good! I didn't care. If I could get home by myself, I could get to rehearsal by myself. She didn't want to be around me, and I didn't need her anyway.

As the train sped along, I looked at the people around me. First, I looked for a Transit Police officer, but I didn't see one. Mom had told me a long time ago, when I first started walking to school on my own, "If you ever get in trouble, Mango, or feel afraid, look for the people who will help. There are always people around who are willing to help." So I looked from face to face, but most of them were looking down at their devices, listening to music with their eyes closed, reading books, or just staring off into space. I couldn't tell which of them would want to help. These New York City faces were different from the faces of people where I came from. These seemed to be in a hurry, tense, wary.

As the train continued, people got off and I was able to get a seat. I recognized the stops in Brooklyn: Borough Hall, Nevins Street, Atlantic Avenue . . . I was feeling pretty confident. But after Atlantic Avenue, the next few stops were unfamiliar. Franklin Avenue? President Street? Sterling Street? I'd never seen these stops before. I stood up and wobbled across the car to check the subway map.

The map was a series of different colored lines that crisscrossed and zigzagged over the five boroughs of New York City. Between the moving train and all the colors, letters, and numbers, I couldn't figure out where I was.

I took a deep breath and tried to calm down. A lot more people got off when the train stopped at Church Avenue. I needed to find a kind face, the kind of kind face that would want to help.

To my left, there was a group of really tall teen boys. A couple of them were tossing a basketball back and forth across the aisle. Maybe they were a basketball team. They didn't look menacing, but they didn't look helpful either. To my right and farther down, there was an elderly lady with blue-tinted hair. She was clutching a canvas shopping bag on her lap and seemed to be smiling to herself. She had on a hat with a little net that covered the top of her face that reminded me of the old-fashioned lady from the airplane. I decided that she looked like a person who'd want to help me.

As I slid into the seat beside the lady, the train lurched, making me bump into her. High-pitched barking came from the canvas bag, followed by the head of a snarling Chihuahua! I screamed. The old lady screamed. The doors slid open, and the woman trotted off the train, yelling, "Stay away! He'll bite you! Stay away!"

I clutched my chest it was racing so fast. The basketball guys started laughing at me, barking and imitating the old lady. I realized I really sucked at finding a kind face that wanted to help. An announcement crackled from the speaker. "The next and last stop is Flatbush Avenue, Brooklyn College. Last stop on this train. Stand clear of the closing doors, please."

Brooklyn College . . . that sounded familiar. I wondered why and then I realized that was where my mother had gone to college!

A calmness came over me. I ignored those boys' mocking laughs down at the other end of the car. I had a connection to this stop. This was a place that had been important in my mother's life, and now, that's where I found myself going. I knew what I needed to do. I would get off, leave the train station, and call Mom. She'd give me directions to get back to Aunt Zendaya's. Or I could call Aunt Zendaya and she would come and get me!

The speaker crackled, "Flatbush Avenue, Brooklyn College. This is the last stop on this train." I got off and headed up the stairs to the exit.

Coming up out of the subway, it felt as though my eyes weren't big enough to take in all the activity going on around me. Buses were rolling by, cars, taxis whizzing past, bicycles dodging in and out of traffic, horns blaring. There were shops everywhere—retail stores, restaurants, fruit and vegetable stands, food trucks. Songs in different languages blasted from speakers in front of the different storefronts. People, mostly black and brown, hurried this way and that, carrying packages, pushing children in strollers. Students headed to and from the college, some on skateboards, scooters, or bikes. I turned around in circles, trying to take it all in.

I looked at the intersection where so many people were crossing the streets in different directions or waiting for the lights to change from red to green. *This is the place where my mother's life changed!* I had to call her, not just to help me find my way back to Aunt Z's, but I needed to share this moment with her. To tell her I was here, and I could feel her presence with me.

I took out my phone and pressed the home key to make it light up, but it didn't. I pressed again. Nothing. I tried to turn it off and then on again. That usually worked when something weird was going on, but it didn't respond—it was just plain dead. Then I remembered face2facing with Izzy and the low battery warning. I completely forgot to charge my phone when I got back to rehearsal! Now here I was, stranded, with a phone I couldn't use!

I felt tears welling up inside me, but no—I was not going to cry at this huge intersection with hundreds of people rushing by me. *Think, Mango, think!* There must have been some way to contact people before there were cell phones. Of course–a phone booth! Wasn't there one on every corner? I looked around, but there was not one phone booth in sight. Where did they put them nowadays? I began to walk down Flatbush Avenue, looking all around me. I had to find one before it got dark. I was doing my best to be brave, but it was way harder to be brave as it got dark.

After walking three blocks, I still couldn't find a phone booth, and it was getting close to twilight. I stopped on a corner for a minute, trying to calm myself, when I heard Bob Marley's voice. He was singing "Three Little Birds," Dada's favorite Bob Marley song, and mine. I loved the way it made me feel everything was going to be all right.

I continued walking down the street, trying to figure out where the song was coming from, and found a West Indian bakery. I walked toward the music and as I got closer, the smell of beef patties beckoned me inside—it was as if I were at home. Looking up at the menu, I saw they had patties, oxtail stew, brown stew fish and turn cornmeal, jerk chicken and jerk pork, escovitch fish, plantain tarts, stew peas, bun and cheese, ackee, and saltfish . . . all foods I loved, and that my Dada cooked for me. I couldn't help it, tears began to fall from my eyes—big, bowling-ball-size tears of relief.

There was a woman behind the counter, stout but fit, with kind brown eyes and a warm smile. She looked at me and said, "What wrong, child? Why ya cry fa?" Her accent made the tears fall even faster. She was from Jamaica, no doubt about it. She was Jamaican, just like my Dada.

The woman came from around the counter, sat down at one of the few tables, and patted the seat beside her. "Come here, gal. Come tell Miss Clover what a gwan?"

I sat beside her and spilled everything that had happened since Zippy let me get on the wrong train. Miss Clover said, "If you want to get to Bergen Street, you have to take the 2 train, not the 5. Me can't believe that gal would send you off on the wrong train like that." She pulled out her phone. "Let's call your auntie, so she can come fetch ya."

Unfortunately, I never memorized Aunt Z's phone number. It was programmed into my phone, so I didn't think I had to.

Wrong! But I did know Dada's and Mom's phone numbers by heart. I gave her Dada's number, because Mom sometimes had a hard time understanding a thick Jamaican accent, especially when she was upset—as I knew she would be when she found out what had happened.

Miss Clover dialed the number and put her phone on speaker. Dada picked up immediately. "Hello?"

"Allo?"

"Hi, Dada."

"Mango? Are you okay? Whose phone is this? Where are you?"

"I'm fine, Dada. I'm with Miss Clover at her bakery."

"What? We been worried about you! Your aunt called and said you were late and she couldn't get you on the phone and that gal that take to you rehearsal not answering her phone or returning messages. Who is this Miss Clover?"

"Me is Miss Clover. This my bakery. The child come in frazzled, yes. Tears roll down she face and she tell me about this hard-rice-cookin', duck foot heifer who let her get on the wrong train and make she get lost!"

In the midst of all my drama, I couldn't help but laugh at Miss Clover's description of Zippy. It was a real insult to a Jamaican if you couldn't cook your rice right.

Dada asked, "Mango, how did you come by there?"

"I heard Bob Marley singing, and I smelled food just like you cook at home. It made me feel like I had found someone who would want to help me."

Miss Clover hugged me to her bosom. "This a brave and smart lickle girl you have here, suh."

"Yes, me know. And me very proud of she."

Miss Clover gave Dada the address of the bakery, so he could let Aunt Zendaya know where to pick me up. He also suggested we not tell Mom about what happened just yet. He would break it to her gently, later, when she got home from work. "You know your mother. She grow wings and talons and fly up there and give that Zippy gal what for."

"I know, Dada," I giggled.

While I waited for Aunt Zendaya, Miss Clover stuffed me with the best Jamaican food I'd had, next to Dada's. I told her about the *Yo, Romeo!* and why I was in New York. She was very impressed. As customers came through, she would point to me and exclaim, "Me got a movie star at me table, eating me food!"

When Aunt Zendaya arrived, she couldn't resist eating whatever was vegan on the menu—the stew peas and plantain tarts were her favorite. She bought a bunch of our favorites to take back with us.

When we got back to the apartment, I was so tired and full of good-good food, I crawled into bed without even taking my clothes off. But I did remember to plug in my phone to charge it. I wouldn't be caught unprepared again.

CHAPTER TWENTY-TWO

Mom Blasts Off!

I n the morning, as I was getting ready, I went over my
route to get to rehearsal. I was a little worried about doing
it alone, but I had learned my lesson yesterday—always be
aware of where you're going and how to get there. There
would be no more getting on the wrong train ever again!

I picked up my phone and turned it on, one hundred
percent charged. That was another lesson yesterday's
experience taught me—always keep your phone charged!
When my phone was back on, I saw I had a series of missed
calls from Mom. Uh-oh. I figured I'd better get this over with
now, so I face2faced her.

"Mango!"

"Hi, Mom. Sorry I didn't answer your calls last night."

"That's okay, baby. Zendaya told me you were fast asleep,
and after your ordeal, who could blame you."

"I'm sorry," I said again.

"Don't be. It wasn't your fault. That Zipper girl, she better
thank her lucky stars that I wasn't close enough to snatch
her bald-headed!"

Uh-oh. That was an example of her Brooklyn coming out. "Mom, relax. It's okay."

"Oh, honey, it's better than okay. After your father told me what happened, I called Mr. Bob and gave him a piece of my mind he will never forget."

"But he didn't do anything wrong!"

"Yes, he did. He told us we could trust that spiteful sister of his. I want her fired."

"Mom, you can't do that!"

"I told him to fire her or else I was coming up to New York to bring you home today."

"Mom, I have a contract. . ."

"I have a contract, too. I'm contracted to keep you safe and not leave you in the hands of fools. That's my contract, and there ain't no way I'm ever gonna break it."

Wow, Mom really was on the warpath. I had to find a way to calm her down. "Mom, I'm okay. Really. I took your advice and looked for someone to help, and I found her—Miss Clover. And I got off the train at Brooklyn College, because I remembered what you told me about running track there and the place where you had the accident. It felt like you there with me, and it calmed me down."

"Aw, baby, you know I will always be there for you, whether I know I'm needed or not," Mom said. "I called that Miss Clover and thanked her and told her if I ever get back to Brooklyn, I'm gonna hug her neck."

I laughed. "That's nice, Mom. Um, is Bob really going to fire Zippy?"

"He said he'd talk to you about it before making a final decision, but I hope he does."

"But she's his *sister*, Mom."

"Yeah, well . . . I guess I know what it's like having a butter-headed sister, but still, well, since it was an accident."

"What was an accident?"

"You two getting separated in the crowd. She swears it was an accident."

Zippy said it was an accident? She was trying to cover her tracks and save her job! I mean, who smiled and waved at someone they just *accidentally* separated from? But if I told my mother what had really happened, my phone might explode, so I said, "Okay. I have to get ready to go to rehearsal. I can go on my own now."

"Oh, no you don't. You sit tight. Mr. Bob said he was sending . . . um . . . somebody with a strange name, but he promised me he or she was way more reliable than that Zipper or whatever her name is."

"But Mom, I know the way!"

"Don't 'but Mom' me, unless you want me to come up there and get you today."

I sighed. "Ooookay. Bye, Mom."

"Bye, honey. I love you."

"Love you back."

I hung up and started to get ready, wondering who my new escort would be. Maybe it was Roz, the actress who was worried she was too young to play my mother. I kind of hoped it wasn't, but she'd still be a lot better than Zippy.

I was about to take a bite of one of the plantain tarts we brought home last night when the buzzer rang from downstairs—a half hour earlier than Zippy's usual pickup time. It wasn't the signal she had come up with, so I buzzed whoever it was in, and waited to open the door to my Mystery Escort.

I was tugging a scrunchie on my hair to make my daily Afro puff when there was a knock at the door. Aunt Zendaya, her hair bonnet lopsided on her head, looked up sleepily and asked, "Who's that knocking?"

"Must be my new escort."

"Oh yeah, your mama told me somebody new was coming today."

I went to the door, opened it, and to my surprise, there stood Acorn! Aunt Zendaya screamed and dove under the bedclothes. I almost laughed, but I was more shocked that Acorn was there. I said, "Hi. What are you doing here?"

Acorn smiled, puzzled, "Didn't you get my texts?"

"Uh...no." Then I remembered I had turned my phone off the night before.

"After the drama of last night, I volunteered to take Zippy's place. But it would mean leaving earlier every day and staying later . . . if you don't mind."

From under the covers we heard, "She don't mind." Aunt Zendaya peered out, adjusting her bonnet. "Do you, baby?"

I smiled. "Nope, I don't mind at all." The day was starting off pretty good. Even though I had to go through getting lost in Brooklyn yesterday, today I had the escort I wanted, so all's well that ends well!

Acorn and I chatted on our way to the subway. "I hope I didn't embarrass your aunt."

"Maybe a little bit, but she'll get over it, I'm sure."

"How sure?"

"Very. She likes you."

He beamed. "Really? You think so?"

Uh-oh. Maybe I had said too much. I was not supposed to get involved in grown folks' love lives, but it seemed like the feelings were mutual, so I said, "I know so. She had a million questions about you. Questions I couldn't answer, because I don't even know you that well."

His entire face lit up. "I have a million questions for her, too."

As we waited on the subway platform, I said, "My mom is really mad at Zippy, but I hope she doesn't get fired."

"I know Bob and Larry take your safety very seriously. Perhaps that is what she deserves."

"But she's Bob's sister and she has a lot of friends in the show. If she gets fired over this, I'm worried everyone will hate me."

"They were not hired to love you. Don't let worry drain

your creative energy. I've worked with Zippy before. She's what you call a 'pot stirrer.' Soon enough everyone will recognize her for who she is. Don't trouble yourself about her or anyone—the universe will handle it."

The train came, and I thought about what he said all the way from Brooklyn into Manhattan. Being a part of this show, even all the way in New York City, Off-Off-Off Broadway, it wasn't much different than middle school. Some people liked you and some didn't. Some were bullies and you just had to learn to handle them, be strong, and trust yourself. So, I made up my mind to focus on the work, not on Gabriel Faust and Zippy. I determined to be the best Juliet I could be. Even better than before. Everything else would take care of itself.

I took out my phone and sent a text to myself:

Remember, u r not a liar. U r a good person. Trust urself and believe in urself. Love, Mango Delight Fuller

CHAPTER TWENTY-THREE

Un-ZIPPY-ed

I t was nice getting to rehearsal early. I helped Acorn set
up the room, and then I had time to stretch, warm up,
and review the dance steps we'd learned the day before. I
felt ready to face whatever came my way. I still had a few
minutes before the rest of the cast arrived, so I went to the
ladies' room to put on some of Aunt Zendaya's lipstick.

I thought I was the only one in the restroom when I
entered, but as I was leaning toward the mirror to put on my
lipstick, the door to a stall opened, and guess who stepped
out?

"Mango."

"Zippy." She went to the sink, turned on the water, got
some soap from the dispenser, and started washing her
hands. "That's a nice shade of lipstick. What's it called?"

I side-eyed her and said, "It's called *lipstick*."

"*Hmm*. Okay. I guess you're mad at me."

I didn't say a word but kept calmly putting on my lipstick.

Zippy went on talking. "Seriously, though, I feel terrible.

173

I worried about you all night. I . . . I . . . it was an accident, I swear!"

I wasn't going to bite my tongue or pretend everything was okay to avoid conflict. I had to stop doing that. I'd made that mistake too many times before. "You smiled and wiggled your fingers at me as the train pulled out of the station. It was no accident. I may be young, but I'm not a fool."

"I know. I'm so sorry. I was just so . . . See? I can't stand it when people lie to me!"

"I was following instructions. Frances Francisco told me to tell you that, to tell everyone that!"

"I know that now. I'm really, really sorry, Mango. Can you forgive me?"

"I don't know."

She put her wet soapy hands together in a pleading gesture. "Please don't make them fire me. You know how much this show means to me. I'm almost thirty-five, remember? This is my last chance."

I couldn't believe I was actually starting to feel sorry for her. I knew Mom wanted her to be fired, but I didn't think that was fair. It would be fair only if she were a terrible actress and singer and didn't do the work, but she was good, funny, and a great belter, too. I wouldn't say she was better than Izzy in the role, but she more than held her own. I didn't think it would be fair to fire her just because she was a jerk to me.

"I'll go back to being your chaperone," she continued, still pleading with her soapy hands. "I'll ask Bob. I'll do it for free—"

"No!" I said it so loud, it kind of echoed in the bathroom. "I'll make you a deal. I'll ask Bob not to fire you if you promise *not* to ask to chaperone me again."

"Oh wow! Thank you, Mango!" She was either a very good actress or truly sincere, because tears were falling from her eyes. "I thought I was done for. Bob was so mad on the phone last night, I thought . . ." She reached up to wipe her tears, forgetting she had soap on her hands and—"Ow! I got soap in my eyes! Ow!"

I left her there splashing water into her eyes thinking to myself, *serves you right!*

When Bob and Larry arrived, they called me out into the hall to speak with them.

Bob said, "Mango, I'm so sorry about your ordeal last night. Are you okay?"

"Yes, I'm fine."

"Zippy losing you like that is inexcusable. I thought she'd be more responsible."

Larry said, "I think we have to let her go."

"No, please don't. She's really good in the show and I like coming in early with Acorn, so . . ."

Bob and Larry looked at each other, then agreed to keep Zippy. I could tell Bob was relieved that all of this didn't lead to even bigger problems with his family. Before we went back in, I said, "Um . . . I'm really sorry for being so late coming back from lunch yesterday."

Bob smiled. "That's okay. We know there were circumstances beyond your control. Besides, you're doing a good job."

"Good?" Larry said, "You're doing great, Mango. You're dancing and singing better than ever. Keep it up."

I felt really good as we went back into the studio.

When TJ arrived, he came directly over to me. He put his backpack down next to my bag, ran his fingers through his Mohawk, and said, "Did you know a group of parrots are called a company?"

Hmm. Obscure facts. He must be feeling anxious. I said, "I didn't know that. Why are you telling me?"

He cleared his throat. "Because, well, all of us in *Yo, Romeo!* are a company, too. And just like parrots, there's a whole lot of chatter. Last night, it was mainly about you."

"I don't care."

"Well, I do. I mean, they were saying things like you were acting like a superstar coming back late from lunch and stuff. Plus the fact that I was a little cold to you yesterday when I was leaving."

"A little cold? More like Frosty the Showman."

He chuckled. "That was so lame."

"I know. Anyway, it was my fault. I'm sorry. I should have said something to you before I left with Gabriel Faust, or at least asked if you could come with us."

"He wouldn't have let me."

"Maybe not, but . . ."

"It's okay, we're cool. And I'm gonna straighten out the rest of the cast about all the things that were being said on the texts."

"Don't."

"But it's not fair and I'm gonna tell 'em."

"No. Don't. I don't need you to stand up for me, TJ. I'm trying to learn to handle my own drama, whether it's in school or here. Show business is hard, so I've got to toughen up. At least, that's what everyone keeps telling me."

TJ nodded and smiled, his kiwi green eyes sparkling. "Okay. That's dope. Do *you*, Queen."

I laughed at the slang he was obviously picking up from his new friends. As he headed away, I called out to him. "Did you know that on average, in their lifetime, an average human will eat seventy assorted insects and ten spiders while sleeping?"

He cringed. "Yuck! The insects I can deal with, but spiders! Is that true?"

I batted my lashes. "Of course! Queens don't lie."

⌣

The day's rehearsal went as smooth as whipped butter. I had no interaction with Zippy unless we were in a scene together. When it came to Gabriel Faust, I acted like nothing had happened and so did he. He didn't apologize for ghosting me, and I didn't need him to. I was as nice to him as I would be to anyone and concentrated on my work. Also, I decided I would call him Gabriel, not Faustie. I didn't consider myself a part of his "squad," and I didn't want to be—not anymore.

I had lunch with TJ and the other teen cast members he'd hung out with yesterday when I stood him up. They were all around the same age as we were and played our friends in the show. LaRon was a freckle-faced clown with long locs and hair shaved clean on both sides, Claxton was one of the lead dancers, Chelsea was an amazing singer, and Chanté I found out was my understudy. They had all moved to New York from all over the county to go to a professional acting middle school in the heart of Broadway. All four of them were serious about making it in show business and knew each other from school and auditions.

I was shy and they were a little standoffish at first, but TJ helped us all relax and before long, we were laughing and throwing shade at each other like we were old friends. It was nice getting to spend more time with kids close to my age. They even invited me to join their group text—Yo, Shady-O! We made plans to have sleepovers and spend our days off together. I guess Acorn was right—my comfort zone was getting bigger and it finally felt like I was starting to belong.

CHAPTER TWENTY-FOUR

That's What Besties Are For

When Acorn and I arrived at Aunt Zendaya's that evening, she was sitting on the stoop, dressed in saffron-colored robes. Her skin glistened in the orange sundown light. She had a thermos of iced ginger tea sweetened with agave and offered each of us a cup. We gladly accepted and sat down to join her.

"Sitting on the stoop takes me back to a time when my life was so simple and free," Aunt Zendaya said, taking a sip of her delicious tea. "That's why I chose to live in this old prewar building. Newer buildings don't have stoops like these. They don't have places for people to mingle and become more than just neighbors. The stoop is a place where we can chat and grow and become a community."

"Did you and Mom have a stoop growing up?" I asked.

Aunt Zendaya nodded, telling us about how they would sit on their building's stoop in the summer evenings when the sun and temperature were going down. They'd greet their neighbors, gossip, and joke with their friends. When the streetlights came on, that was the signal to go inside for dinner.

I asked Aunt Zendaya questions about growing up with Mom, and she griped about the perils of having a bossy older sister, but in a funny way. Still, I hoped Jasper wouldn't feel that way about growing up with me.

Acorn told us about his family, that his grandparents had emigrated from Vietnam when his father was very young. Acorn's father adjusted to life in the U.S. quickly, rebelling against his parents and their cultural traditions. I guess it'd take a rebel to name your kids Maple Leaf, Branch, and Acorn. "I wish I were more connected to my Vietnamese heritage," Acorn confessed. "My dad doesn't really understand, but I've been talking more to my grandparents recently. I know that I'm Vietnamese, but it hasn't been easy to figure out how that fits with other parts of my identity, to figure out who I am."

Aunt Zendaya threw her hands up in the air. "Tell me about it! When I changed my name, my sister called me foolish and still refuses to remember to call me by my chosen name."

I piped up, "Mom says that's because you changed your name so many times."

"Of course I did. I was trying to find myself. It took a while for me to grow into Zendaya. And who knows, I might grow into someone with a different name down the road. I don't have a problem with that."

"I might change my name someday, if I find one that suits me better," Acorn mused.

Aunt Zendaya said, "I think Acorn is a lovely name."

Acorn smiled. "You do?"

"Yes, it's unique. Like you."

Sitting next to them as they continued to talk, I felt like I was in a movie—with the camera moving past me to zoom in on the two of them. But I didn't mind not being the star of this show. When the streetlights started to come on, I decided to go in and let the two of them have time to get to know each other. I smiled to myself as I climbed the stairs. Wouldn't it be amazing if Aunt Zendaya met the love of her life all because of me? I could hear my mother now, "Well, well, well, nuts of a feather flock together."

Aunt Zendaya had mentioned that there was a pot of soup on the stove. I wasn't excited by the notion of another flavorless meal, but a girl had to eat, so I heated the pot, ladled a bowl, and tasted the most fantastic soup I've ever had in my life. It was a vegetable medley with corn, carrots, potatoes, celery, okra, squash, and spices that made this magical mixture come to life! Maybe eating cruelty-free wasn't all bad. I needed to ask her for the recipe so I could make it for Dada when I went back home.

After gorging myself on two bowls, I curled up on the couch and face2faced Izzy. As soon as she appeared on my screen, I launched into everything that was going on—Aunt Zendaya and Acorn, the blowup with Zippy, getting abandoned and lost on the subway, my new friends, and the Yo, Shady-O text group. I repeated some of the shady jokes we had made, but then I realized Izzy wasn't laughing. "Guess you had to be there," I said.

"Yes," Izzy said, "I really would rather be there, or in the upside down, or literally anywhere else would be better than being stuck here with my evil doppelgänger cousin."

"Doppel-*what*?"

"Doppelgänger, like a double of yourself that maybe lives in another dimension or is just evil."

"Oh. I'm sorry."

Izzy mocked me, "*Oh, I'm sorry!* I don't need your being sorry, Mango. That doesn't help."

"And you being mean doesn't help either."

We were both silent for a long time. Izzy covered her phone so I couldn't see her face, but I heard her crying. I said, "Izzy? What happened? What's going on? Talk to me!"

"I can't. I gotta go."

"No, wait. Please talk to me. Where is Carmella?"

"She went to a barbecue."

"Why didn't you go with her?"

"I wasn't invited."

"Oh. Who invited Carmella?"

"Hector Osario!"

"WHAT!" That was the boy Izzy had been crushing on all summer!

Izzy's face reappeared on screen, drenched in tears. "I

took Carmella to the park to play handball. She saw him. Went over and started talking to him and batting her eyes. This was after I told her how much I liked him, and how I'd been trying to get his attention all summer. And then he invited *her* to the barbecue."

She started sobbing again.

"Izzy," I started. "I'm so—" No, I wasn't going to say *sorry* again. "Listen, when Marcelle sees Hector with another girl, she's going to use her gel tips to scratch her eyes out."

"No, she won't," Izzy sniffled. "She broke up with him last week. She already has a new boyfriend, a barber next door to her mother's nail salon. OMGZ, Mango, I want to kill her."

"Marcelle?"

"No! Carmella."

"Izzy, calm down."

"This is all your fault."

"My fault?"

"If you hadn't left, I wouldn't have needed Carmella to be my paddleball partner and she would've never met Hector. You're my best friend, and you've ruined my life."

"No way! Your life is not ruined. Carmella will be gone soon, and you'll get your chance with Hector."

"After he's kissed Carmella? Oh no, I don't want no parts of no boy whose lips have touched the body snatcher!"

"Stop!" I burst out laughing. I was relieved when Izzy started laughing, too.

"Hey, thanks," Izzy said.

"For what?"

"For listening. I had to get a lot off my chest and I needed my friend. I was mad when I couldn't get in touch with you last night."

"My phone died . . ."

"And you had a terrible, horrible day and night and blah, blah, blah . . . It doesn't matter, you're here now. Sorry I yelled at you."

"So what, you yelled, that's what besties are for."

We kept chatting until Aunt Zendaya came upstairs around eleven. I was exhausted from laughing at all the different ways Izzy kept imagining how she could rid herself of Carmella. I think I was still giggling as I fell asleep.

CHAPTER TWENTY-FIVE

The Care and Feeding of the Diva

We rehearsed *Yo, Romeo!* six days a week, and it was fun, but also exhausting. When I was in the play at school, we rehearsed for two, maybe three hours after school, then I got to go home. Rehearsing for eight to ten hours a day was brutal! Some nights, my feet hurt so badly when I got home, Aunt Zendaya had to show me how to soak them in hot water and Epsom salt to get some relief.

Once, in the middle of the night, I woke up screaming. Both of my legs were cramping! It was so painful. Thank goodness Aunt Zendaya was there to give me salt water to drink. It was disgusting, but at least it made the cramps go away. My friend Chelsea told me pickle juice was a good remedy for cramping, so I bought a big jar of pickles and kept them in the fridge. Good thing I liked pickles, so they wouldn't go to waste.

The more I worked with Gabriel Faust, the more I realized he was as far from my fantasy BCF as possible. He always arrived late, with Frances Francisco making excuses for him—he had a late recording session; he did a meet-and-greet for charity and his fans wouldn't let him go; there was a photo session for a fashion magazine spread and that took hours!

When he finally *did* show up, he was usually unprepared. We had to do scenes and songs over and over because he couldn't remember his lines. When he was on TV, he didn't have to memorize lines. If he made a mistake, they'd just call, "cut!" and do the scene again until they got it right, which I think made him lazy as an actor. It was weird. Once I thought he was the cutest boy on the planet, but the more I got to know him, the more his good looks seemed to fade away— and the more I dreaded having to kiss him onstage. He was always whining and complaining about something. "Why is it so hot in here?" "Turn down the AC, it's bad for my voice." "Does everyone have to watch us rehearse? Clear the room!"

When he wasn't in a scene, he would leave with Josh and sit in his SUV until he was needed. Acorn would have to call downstairs to get him, and then it would take at least twenty minutes before his majesty would arrive. I started getting headaches and stomachaches whenever I had to rehearse a scene with him. I dreaded the day when I would actually have to kiss him. I tried my best to stay positive and not talk bad about him to my Yo, Shady-O friends, but I didn't think I was fooling them. TJ and Chanté had to stay in the room when we rehearsed, because they were our understudies, so they saw all the madness going down anyway.

The absolute worst day was at the end of the second week of rehearsal. It had been a long week, and Gabriel hadn't even been there the last day and a half. Now he was running late, as usual, so Larry suggested TJ and I rehearse "Duet Forever." It was my favorite song in the show, because I really got to belt and hit the high notes like Beyoncé, and TJ's voice was amazing when his high notes with a hard rock edge would reach the stratosphere. So we were singing our hearts out, having fun, when Gabriel finally arrived. He stood by the door, sulking, as the cast left the room so we could have a *private* rehearsal.

Bob asked us to start with the dialogue at the top of the scene and then go right into the song. We were supposed to be in a recording studio where our characters first meet and fall in love—kind of like the balcony scene in *Romeo and Juliet*. We started the scene, but Gabriel wasn't following the blocking that had been set the week before. He kept walking farther and farther upstage, meaning that to see and talk to him, I couldn't face where the audience would be.

A couple of minutes into the scene, Bob finally spoke up. "Gabe, stick to the blocking, please."

"Don't call me Gabe. I hate that."

Bob's face reddened a little, but he stayed calm. "What would you like me to call you? Gabriel?"

"You can call me Mr. Faust."

My stomach started aching, my emotional mango pit getting larger and heavier by the second. I glanced at TJ and

Chanté, who rolled their eyes. Bob's face got even redder. He said, "Okay, Mr. Faust, I would like you to stick to the blocking that we rehearsed last week."

"What's wrong with what I'm doing now? It's more natural."

"You're upstaging Mango, that's what's wrong with it."

"What are you talking about?"

Bob took a deep breath, stood, and came from behind the table. "When you go so far upstage, she has to turn her back to the audience to see you and talk to you."

"So? Just shoot her from over my shoulder."

"We can't *shoot* her from over your shoulder. There are no cameras here. This isn't a TV show. It's a play, a musical that will be performed on a stage where the audience won't be able to spin around behind you so they can see her."

Gabriel turned purple, realizing how foolish he looked. He walked close to Bob and glared at him. "I still think your blocking stinks. It's boring. Make it better."

"The blocking works fine, and you'd realize that if you'd stick to it."

"You're not the boss of me."

"I'm the director."

"Yeah? Well . . ." He stomped his elevated shoes over to the door, pausing only to order Acorn to call his manager. "Tell her to meet me at the car. We'll see who's in charge around here." The door slammed shut behind him.

Bob balled his fist and turned around in circles as if

he were looking for something or someone to punch. Larry jumped up from the piano and ran to him. "Hey, take it easy. Come on, calm down. Take some deep breaths."

I realized I was shaking. TJ came over and put his arms around me, trying to calm me down. Even though Gabriel had been pretty consistently awful in rehearsals, I'd never been in a situation like that before. Some of the cast started to peek in, trying to find out what was going on. Acorn called for a lunch break, even though it was only eleven o'clock.

TJ, Chanté, and I joined the rest of the Yo, Shady-O crew for lunch, and Gabriel's outburst was all we could talk about.

"That boy is the biggest diva I've ever worked with," LaRon said. "And I was a backup dancer in a Mariah Carey video, mmkay! We all know Madame Carey can carry on!"

"She's the mother of all divas," Chanté agreed.

Claxton said, "If she's the mother, Faustie must be the father!"

Chelsea chimed in, laughing, "Father? More like bratty little brother."

TJ did a perfect imitation of Gabriel as Romper—"Brats rule, fools drool!" We all cracked up. I knew it wasn't very nice to talk about Gabriel behind his back, but I needed to laugh to let out the stress. A part of me was afraid to go back after lunch. Which Gabriel would show up, the charmer who had ghosted me? The silent insecure star behind the oversize sunglasses? Or the diva monster from this morning?

On our way back into the building, Frances Francisco

appeared out of nowhere. She stopped me at the elevators. "We need to talk."

When the elevator doors opened, she led me in and put her hand out to my friends to stop them from getting on, too—"Privacy, please." The door slid closed and she pressed the button for the sixteenth floor. "Listen, Gabriel wants Bob fired. Thoughts?"

I was stunned. My stomach started hurting all over again. "Fired?"

"He says Bob humiliated him in front of the whole cast."

"The whole cast wasn't even in the room, just me, Gabriel, and our understudies."

"What did Bob do?"

"Nothing. He just asked Gabriel to do the blocking that was set last week, and Gabriel refused. Bob didn't yell at him or anything. He just corrected Gabriel, who thought there would be cameras or something."

Frances Francisco sighed deeply. "Okay. Look, sometimes my little star needs a swift kick in the pants. Here's what we'll do. I'm going to take him away for a mental health day, so he can regroup. Tomorrow is a day off, and we'll start again on Monday."

The elevator doors slid open at the sixteenth floor and I stepped out, but Frances Francisco didn't. "By the way," she said, "I spoke to Larry about lowering the key on all of Gabriel's songs. It'll only affect you on the duets, but I'm sure you can handle it. See you next week." The doors closed and she was gone.

The rest of the day was hard, to say the least. Bob was uptight and his fuse was pretty short. He did his best to appear normal, but the rumor about his getting fired was being whispered all around the room. We ended rehearsal two hours early. Bob made a short speech before he let us go.

"Hey everyone, thanks for a great week. It's been a little challenging, but the road to Broadway was never smooth. Get some rest tomorrow, because we have a lot of catching up to do. Keep the gossip down and your spirits up. I love you all. Now get out of here!"

I was drained—mentally, physically, and emotionally. When I got back to Aunt Zendaya's apartment, I saw Izzy had texted me. She wanted me to call her. But I shut off my phone because I didn't want to text, talk, or think about what happened at rehearsal today. I let Aunt Z and Acorn take me on a long run in Prospect Park and then to a movie, where I promptly fell fast asleep.

CHAPTER TWENTY-SIX

Summer in the City

Hoooray for days off! Summer in New York City was everything I thought it would be and more. Yes, it was hot, sticky, and humid, but the excitement of the Big Apple made it all worthwhile. The cast had bonded, especially TJ, LaRon, Claxton, Chelsea, Chanté, and I. We worked hard, and we played even harder! Did we rest on our days off as we had been advised to do? Of course not!

The Yo Shady-O crew took TJ and me under their wing. They showed us all around the city, which practically glistened in the summer light. We went to Central Park, the Museum of Natural History, and the Bronx Zoo. I loved the outdoor concert series at Lincoln Center. I saw an opera, *Aida*, and actually loved it! We had standing room tickets to see *Wicked* and *The Lion King* on Broadway (the best we could afford), and I even won a student rush lottery, so TJ and I got to see *Hamilton!*

Back at rehearsal, lunches were a laugh riot. LaRon was a living, breathing cartoon. With his expressive face and the way he moved, you'd think he could squash and stretch like an animated TV character. Claxton was more reserved, but he had a sly wit that could make you laugh while thinking *if that wasn't so funny, it would be hurtful!*

The girls, Chanté (my understudy) and Chelsea, were like my big sisters. Sometimes we'd go window shopping on our lunch breaks or after rehearsal when Acorn was working late. At sixteen, Chelsea was the most mature and held us in check if we were about to go off the rails—like the time we were dancing around the edges of the Bethesda Fountain in Central Park, pretending we were in the opening credits of *Friends*, and LaRon fell in. The water wasn't deep, barely up to his knees, but Chelsea turned down the volume on our turn-up, bringing us back to our senses before we headed home.

I was having the time of my life. Mom was worried that I wasn't getting enough rest and scolded Aunt Zendaya for letting me hang out with my new friends and stay up so late on my days off. But the world was spinning so fast and I didn't want to get off. I was enjoying work (when *he who shall not be named* wasn't causing drama), because it didn't seem like work to me. I felt like I laughed all day, and I'll admit, sometimes I laughed too much. In the middle of a serious scene or one of my solos, I'd looked across the room and there LaRon would be flaring his nostrils like a bull in a cartoon, and I couldn't help it, I'd crack up. Bob would look at me, one eyebrow reaching for the ceiling, to remind me to stop playing around and be professional. I did my best, but then again, I was only twelve and a half, and some things were just too funny too be ignored.

I didn't enjoy lowering the keys on our duets, especially *Duet Forever*, my favorite song. I could still sing it, but I couldn't soar up into my Beyoncé range, and that made it less fun. Was I being a diva now? I didn't know, but maybe I wanted to show off a little. I felt like I was being held back and couldn't reach my highest potential, just because Gabriel Faust couldn't sing as well as TJ. His manager even insisted we keep the register lowered when TJ did the songs. That was unfair, but what could we do? It felt like we were being held hostage by a star the producers insisted we cater to because his name would sell tickets.

Destiny Manaconda began to show up at rehearsals whenever she wasn't performing at the Summer Jam concerts across the country. It made me a little nervous at first and I tried not to compare myself to her, but it was hard. She was so glamourous. Her clothes, makeup, powder-puff pink hair, even the way she moved across the room. When she showed up, I started feeling like I did when we first started rehearsals, like a plain-Jane kid who couldn't hold a candle to the rest. Even though I knew she was there to keep Faustie in check, I would find myself comparing myself to her, even when I didn't mean to. Gabriel seemed calmer when she was around. He had somebody to sit with him and go on breaks with him. He never tried to be a part of the cast. It seemed as though he felt we were beneath him. But as long as he kept his diva behavior and tantrums to a minimum, we were relieved.

The third week was so hard. We were doing run-throughs of the entire show two times a day. It was starting to affect my voice. My friends suggested I get a steamer to soothe my vocal cords in the morning and evening. Also, Chanté would meet me in the morning and we would warm up our voices together, before the company warm-up. She had been taking voice lessons for ten years and knew how to keep her voice in good shape. I was grateful for the way she was always volunteering to help and support me even though she was my understudy. I asked Bob if Chanté could play Juliet one night during the run, and he said, "Sure. We'll give Chanté and TJ a performance during the last week. I was excited, because I'd actually get to sit in the audience and watch for the first time.

I tried to keep my talking to a minimum when I wasn't at rehearsal. I couldn't afford to stay up all night face2facing with Izzy back at home or with Hailey Joanne across the Atlantic. I texted them when I could, but I seriously needed my rest. I was beginning to realize that an actor and singer's body was her instrument, and you had to almost live like a monk when you were not onstage or in rehearsal. This was really hard for us kids, but when our voices got hoarse or we pulled a muscle, we learned to take care of ourselves the hard way.

For our final week of rehearsal, we moved into a theater on the Lower East Side of Manhattan called The Pure Space. Out front was a large poster featuring Gabriel Faust in his Romeo costume. My friends said I should have been on the poster too, but I didn't mind. Gabriel Faust was the name that sold tickets; it was only fair he be featured. No one knew who I was . . . yet.

The theater was what you'd call intimate, with about ninety-nine seats. It was a bit dusty and musty, but it felt as grand as Radio City Music Hall to me. There was an orchestra pit and more lights than we ever had at Trueheart's auditorium. There was a green room where the actors could hang out. I don't know why they called it a "green" room when the walls were gray cinderblock, but I guess it sounded better than "the gray room." There were two "star" dressing rooms just offstage and three flights of cramped dressing rooms to share, but still, it was glamorous to me.

TJ, LaRon, Claxton, Chelsea, Chanté, and I took the dressing room on the top floor, because we figured we could make as much noise and be as silly as we wanted away from the rest of the company. I could have used the second star dressing room, but I knew I'd be lonely next door to Gabriel Faust. I wanted to be with my friends, no matter how cramped the space.

It felt like the cast was divided into three separate groups. There were the "kids," which I was a part of. We were giddy with excitement about being in a professional show, a show that could move to Broadway and beyond. Then there were the "veterans," or adults. Zippy and Roz seemed to be the leaders of this group; they'd all been in lots of shows and although they were hopeful of going to Broadway too, their enthusiasm seemed muted compared to ours. Last but not least, there was Gabriel Faust, his agents, managers, personal assistants, publicist, stylist, barber, driver, and his bae, Destiny Manaconda, who spent most of her time in Gabriel Faust's dressing room with the rest of his entourage.

Everything seemed to be going well, except when Gabriel Faust started complaining about rehearsing too much. Frances Francisco complained to the producers that he was not only rehearsing the show, but also recording an album at night. So Gabriel Faust was given a lighter rehearsal schedule than the rest of us. That was okay with me, because when he wasn't around, TJ got to step in as Romeo and the band would revert the songs to their original keys—when the cat's away, the band will play! It felt like old times back at Trueheart Middle School.

The sets and costumes for this production were a humongous step up from what we had in middle school. At Trueheart we had just one painted backdrop for many different scenes and some set pieces built by the shop department. Here there were actual sets–of Juliet's bedroom, a recording studio, a lavish nightclub, and the kind of places pop stars would hang at. The costumes were rented, but from a rental company that furnished actual Broadway shows, so they were lavish to the max. I felt like a real star, draped in sequins, rhinestones, and bugle-beaded gowns. I couldn't wait for my parents to see me in the show.

As opening night got closer and closer, I was uber excited—not only because of the show, but Hailey Joanne was coming to see me! She and her mother were flying in from Paris to do fittings for her mother's vow-renewal ceremony, which meant they would be in the city for opening night. Hailey Joanne had already decided that I would spend a few nights in their penthouse suite at the Saint Voltaire, only the most exclusive hotel in Manhattan. Gabriel Faust had a suite there, too.

I had a late call the day before Hailey Joanne was set to arrive, because I had to go to the doctor. Everyone had to do this in case someone became ill and we had to cancel performances—insurance stuff, I guess. I had been putting it off since I'd arrived, but with opening night almost upon us, the producers asked Aunt Zendaya to take me that morning.

Anywho, when Aunt Zendaya and I got to the theater around eleven-thirty, I was stunned as I entered the stage door. Someone was singing my favorite song in the show, "Duet Forever," with Gabriel Faust—in the original key! She sounded great. In fact, to my ears she sounded better than me.

Watching from the wings, I saw it was Destiny Manaconda onstage. *She* was singing my duet with Gabriel Faust. They were staring deep into each other's eyes, filling the music with such passion that the cast sitting in the audience was gawking at them in amazement.

I wanted to slip out of the theater unnoticed, but Aunt Zendaya, maybe sensing my feelings of self-doubt and embarrassment, put her arm around my shoulder.

At the end of the song, they kissed passionately, and everyone burst into applause and cheers. Even my Yo, Shady-O friends were snapping their fingers, shouting, "Yaaasss, diva!" and "You did that gurrrll!" and "You better saaannnnggg!"

I was frozen in the wings, stage right. Destiny Manaconda was a star. If she were in the show with Gabriel Faust, it would definitely be a hit, because she was perfect. I was just plain old Mango.

Bob leapt onstage noticing Aunt Zendaya and me. "Look who's here!" he called out in his loudest voice, as if clueing everyone in on my presence. He took my hand and led me onstage. "Our star has arrived! Mango, good to have you back. How'd it go?"

I had no voice. A series of padlocks had snapped shut along my windpipe and no sound came out. "Everything went fine," Aunt Zendaya spoke up. "She aced the physical, of course."

"Of course! We knew she would. No doubt about that," Bob said, clearing his throat. He ran his fingers nervously through his rust-colored hair. "We were just having a little fun here. Faustie wanted to run the song and since Mango wasn't here, who better to run through it with him?"

Aunt Zendaya said, "How about Mango's understudy? Doesn't she have one? It's Chanté, if I'm not mistaken."

The moment was awkward to the extreme, and the room was so quiet you could hear the lights buzzing quietly up above. I glanced over to where Chanté was sitting in the front row, next to TJ and the rest of our crew. Her eyes seemed sad for me as she shrugged and glanced down at the floor. On stage, Gabriel was whispering into Destiny Manaconda's ear as she checked her makeup in a jewel-encrusted compact mirror. I felt like a ghost in a movie, one that you could see right through. All the confidence I had been building the last couple weeks of rehearsal was suddenly gone, and I was just the little girl in the mirror, out of her element all over again.

When Acorn called for a five-minute break, I immediately headed for the dressing room. As I hurried up the winding staircase, I wasn't sure how I was feeling. I felt as though someone had thrown a bucket of cold water on my face, making me realize I was not as good as I thought I was. Still, I was proud of how Aunt Zendaya stood up for me. For a moment, she was like my own personal Frances Francisco. Then there was another side of me, a side I had been working on since I started in my school's production of *Yo, Romeo!* This side of me was trying to learn to assert herself and she said, *Yes, I may be only twelve and a half years old, but I'm stronger than I've ever been, and I'm NOT giving up my part in the show!*

I stopped myself at the dressing room door. I didn't really need to go in. I had come there to hide or maybe even cry, but no. That was the old Mango. The new Mango was going to go right back onstage and stand her ground. Why should I feel less than Destiny Manaconda? So what if she looked and acted like a star. I could do that too, if I really wanted to—and I decided that I did. That's how I would build my confidence back up. I would show them all that I could be glamorous, exciting, and mature when I wanted to be. Luckily, the perfect ally was on her way to New York. If anyone could help with my transformation, it was Hailey Joanne Pinkey. I was not going to hold back. Not now or ever again.

CHAPTER TWENTY-SEVEN

A Castle in the Sky

I made it through the rest of rehearsal by taking my mom's advice—fake it until you make it. Yes, I was scared and nervous about being compared to a big star like Destiny Manaconda, but I didn't have to let anyone else know it. If I put on a brave face and pretended that I wasn't intimidated, then people would believe I wasn't—and it worked. No one treated me any differently. The Yo, Shady-O crew and I laughed and joked as if nothing out of the ordinary had happened. But on the inside where no one could see my true feelings, I couldn't help but compare myself to Destiny Manaconda. To my mind, she was perfect, and if I wanted to be a star like her, then I had to try to be more like her.

Back at Aunt Zendaya's that evening, I studied everything Destiny Manaconda. I watched all her music videos on YouTube. I read as many of her interviews as I could find. I listened to all her songs, trying to imitate her little trills and the hiccup-like catch she had in her singing voice that

I wished I had in mine. I even went back and watched old episodes of *Cupcakers* to study her mannerisms, the way she looked when she pouted and batted her eyelashes flirtatiously, her wide-eyed "uh-oh" face that always drew laughs from the audience when she was about to cause a hilarious upset. I shut myself in the bathroom, using the mirror to perfect the way she stood when modeling for Calvin Klein. She had talent, charisma, and something I couldn't just pull out of thin air—superstar glam.

Since we had the next day off, the Yo, Shady-O crew was blowing up our group text trying to decide what we should do together. I begged off, telling them my friend was arriving from Paris and I was spending the day with her. TJ texted separately to ask if he could come along. Even though Hailey Joanne had already suggested we do a mini Trueheart reunion, I told him we were having a girls' day. I needed Hailey Joanne all to myself for my Manaconda glamazon makeover.

⁓

Aunt Zendaya's doorbell buzzed a few minutes after noon the next day. The car Hailey Joanne had sent to drive me to the Saint Voltaire had arrived! I grabbed my overnight bag before the buzzing stopped, though Aunt Zendaya made me wait for her to be ready. Even though Mom had assured her the Pinkeys could be trusted, Aunt Zendaya, maybe feeling a bit more protective after what happened the day before at rehearsal, insisted on trekking down from the fourth floor to make sure all was on the up and up.

When we stepped outside the apartment building, there, waiting for me at the back door of a gleaming black SUV, was the Pinkey family chauffeur from back home, Mr. Versey! He was as distinguished as ever, with his jet-black hair and snow-white mustache. His eyes sparkled as he opened the rear passenger door. "Miss Mango, so very happy to see you again."

I couldn't help myself—I gave him a hug and told him how happy I was to see him, too. He introduced himself to Aunt Zendaya, and I could see that she was impressed. Assured that I was in good hands, Aunt Zendaya waved from the stoop as I was whooshed away in the comfort of the Pinkeys' luxury SUV.

As we made our way through the traffic from Brooklyn to the Upper East Side of Manhattan, I told Mr. Versey that I was surprised to see him here in New York. "Why?" he asked. "The Pinkeys always travel with their entourage, of which I am a part." He chuckled. "Working for these rich folks, I've been all over Europe, Africa, India . . . you name it, I've been there. Ms. Altovese wouldn't trust any driver to chauffeur Miss Hailey Joanne and herself but me."

Ms. Altovese Trueheart-Pinkey was Hailey Joanne's mother. She was the most glamorous, sophisticated, and gorgeous woman I had ever met. The granddaughter of

Irma Beth Trueheart, founder of Trueheart Beauty, a line of haircare products for women of color that made her a multimillionaire before she was twenty-five years old. Ms. Altovese oversaw her grandmother's empire all around the world. The only thing that rivaled her beauty was her kindness and good taste. Kindness because she was always so gracious and insisted on calling me by my middle name, Delight. Good taste, because she hired my father to cater Hailey Joanne's birthday celebration the previous spring and her upcoming vow-renewal to her car dealership tycoon husband, Mr. Pinkey.

Mr. Versey went on to tell me that wealthy people like the Pinkeys never traveled alone. They had private jets so they could bring along their entourage, from stylists to cooks to secretaries and assistants. Everyone was on board so the family could be assured of the safety and comfort of home wherever they landed. I gagged. *It must cost a fortune to travel with all of those people*, but then again I thought, *if you're fortunate enough to have a fortune, go on and live your best life!*

The Pinkeys' butler was waiting as Mr. Versey pulled the SUV up to a private entrance at the back of the hotel. He was a butler and his actual name was Mr. Butler. I used to think this was very funny, but he took himself so seriously that I tried to keep my jokes about it to myself. Mr. Butler the butler led me to a private elevator at the back of the impressively understated lobby. The express elevator to the penthouse felt like I was traveling through one of the portkeys in Harry Potter, causing my stomach to drop to my knees as we were rocketed to the eighty-eighth floor.

The elevator doors opened, and for the second time in my Hailey Joanne experience, my eyes popped at the grandeur in front of me. The entry hall had a three-story vaulted glass ceiling that filled the space with light that gleamed off the marble floor. There were fresh-cut orchid arrangements everywhere, their fragrance delicately scenting the air around me. It was a castle in the sky, high above the city.

Mr. Butler the butler informed me that there were six king-size bedrooms, four queen-size bedrooms, all with en suites (their own bathrooms!); a dining room for twelve, two powder rooms, two wet bars, and a library up a winding staircase that led to a wrap-around deck, from which you could see a three hundred sixty degree panorama view of Manhattan. I wasn't sure why he was telling me all this until he took out a tablet that had a layout of the space and asked, "Which bedroom would you prefer, Miss Mango?"

I gulped and told him I'd like the one closest to Hailey Joanne. He touched the screen and highlighted an adjoining room, asking if it would be satisfactory. I grinned and said, "Satisfactory and then some!" Stone-faced, he led me through the penthouse to the bedroom wing. All of the walls, furnishings, carpets, and hardwood floors were in shades of white, off-white, gray, and beige. Peeking into one of the open rooms, I saw a red accent wall and an elaborate area rug to match. It was all so tasteful and elegant. I felt out of place with my jeans, sneakers, and faux vintage Freddie Mercury T-shirt.

He stopped in front of a door, opened it, and turned to me. "Miss Hailey Joanne is experiencing a severe case of jet lag and is still in bed. Make yourself comfortable and she'll be with you in a few hours, I'm sure." With that, he turned on his heel and went back down the hall without making a sound.

I stepped into the room, which was as white, gray, beige, and elegant as the rest of the penthouse. The king-size bed was massive! I dropped my overnight bag, ran across the room, and did a grand jeté leap onto it. I felt like I'd landed on a cloud in the heavens, especially after sharing a futon with Aunt Z for the previous few weeks. As I lay there, I thought back to what Mr. Butler the butler had said . . . Hailey Joanne would be with me in a few hours? No way! I sat up, looked around, and spied the door that adjoined Hailey Joanne's room. I headed toward it, determined to wake Hailey Joanne from her transatlantic stupor. We had a LOT of work to do if we were going to transform-aconda me into a superstar in one day!

CHAPTER TWENTY-EIGHT

A Star Is Reborn

I knew waking Hailey Joanne would not be easy. She was used to doing things her own way in her own time. Before we became friends, she was the leader of the Cell-belles, a group of snooty girls at our school who shunned anyone without a cellphone. She used to make fun of my name and tease me every chance she got. Hailey Joanne and my ex-best friend forever, Brooklyn, tried to humiliate me by signing me up to audition for the school play without my knowledge, but it backfired on them because I got the lead role! Impressed, Hailey Joanne uploaded my audition to YouTube and when I went viral, she and I actually started to talk and become friends.

I approached the door between our rooms and opened it, careful not to make a sound. The door must've been soundproof, because the second I opened it, I was assaulted by a snore that could best a jackhammer in a noise pollution contest.

I entered Hailey Joanne's dark room and stood still, getting my bearings and wondering how I should wake her. I could jump on the bed and say, "Ta-da! I'm here, girlfriend!"

Or I could creep up to the bed, tap her on the shoulder, and say, "Wakey-wakey for goodness sakey!" Then again, I could use the song Dada used to sing to get me out of bed in the morning when I was in elementary school: "Get up, get up, you sleepyhead! Get up, get up, get out of bed!" No, that wouldn't be fair, because I used to bury my head under my pillow and scream to get him to cut it out.

Deciding to take the gentle and quiet approach, I crept up to the massive bed on my tiptoes. Just when I reached her bedside, Hailey Joanne sat straight up and yelled, "Who's there?!" I screamed! She screamed! I backed away from the bed so fast, I fell on my butt. She leapt up so she was standing on the bed, brandishing what I thought was a weapon but turned out to be a remote control. Suddenly the lights came on and there she was, looming over me, her hair standing on end like one of those little troll dolls, her eyes covered by a sleep mask. I screamed again!

Hailey Joanne lifted the mask. She squinted at me and said, "Mango? What in the world . . .?" Relieved, I slumped back on the carpet, and after taking a moment to catch my breath, I started laughing uncontrollably. Then Hailey Joanne started laughing and joined me on the floor. We rolled around, hugging each other and cackling in each other's faces—until I had to pull away and cover my nose. Hailey Joanne asked, "What's wrong?"

"Morning breath, girl. You seriously need to do something about that right away."

She swatted at me playfully and headed toward her en suite. "While I do my toilette, dial nine on the phone and tell Mr. Butler we want dinner for two."

"Dinner? It's only one in the afternoon."

Hailey Joanne posed dramatically with the back of her hand on her forehead. "Sacré bleu, I'm still on Paris time. Order un déjeuner pour deux, s'il vous plaît."

I knew she was just showing off the French lessons she'd been taking all summer, so I just said, "Huh?"

"Oh, mon Dieu!" she giggled. "Pardonnez-moi. Order lunch for two, if you please, while I brush my teeth."

As she headed away, I laughed. "You might want to use a brush on your hair while you're at it, mademoiselle!"

Lunch was epic! Served on the veranda by the waitstaff, we ate Bavarois d'asperges vertes (asparagus mousse with a cumin and coriander mayonnaise and shards of ham), for the main course a cassoulet (a delicious casserole with beans, pork sausage, and chicken breast), a cheese plate, and for dessert, crème brûlée a la confiture (caramel cream with jam). I couldn't believe French people ate so much rich food for lunch, but Hailey Joanne told me, "In France, the midday meal is the biggest meal of the day. Dinner is much lighter and easier to digest before bed."

Whatever the rules were, everything was delicious and I used my phone to take a picture of each beautiful dish to share with Dada, who I knew would appreciate them. Hailey Joanne told me all about her weeks in Paris, the shopping, the sightseeing, and Marc Hervé Guillon, the teen son of her mother's favorite couturier. "He is divine. The perfect gentleman, uber gorgeous, and best of all, as I was boarding our jet to fly home, he hugged me and whispered in my ear, 'Je t'aime.'"

"Really?"

"Yes!"

"What does it mean?"

"It means 'I love you'!"

A big part of me felt relieved that Hailey Joanne was interested in another boy and had moved on from TJ. Spending so much time with him here in New York, I wasn't sure if I still only wanted to be friends with him. I could completely be myself with TJ, and I really liked spending time together. I wasn't sure what that meant, but maybe the needle was moving away from friend-friends toward something more . . . at least for me. I didn't know how he felt. Still, I needed to make sure Hailey Joanne was really moving on, so things wouldn't be weird between us, so I asked, "Did he really mean it? I mean, like was it romantic love or just 'love you like a friend' love?"

"Why would I waste my time telling you about it if it were just 'love you like a friend' love? We went everywhere together. I saw Paris through the eyes of a true Parisien. Mother didn't like it. She wanted the trip to be all about the two of us exploring the city together, but I mean, really? If you had the chance to explore the most romantic city in the world, who would you chose to tour with? Your mother, or a living, breathing, hunk of Brie with broad shoulders, hazel eyes, pouty lips, and an accent to die for?"

I was about to answer when Mrs. Trueheart-Pinkey swept onto the veranda. Hailey Joanne shushed me and shook her head, a quick warning to not continue talking about her crush. Mrs. Trueheart-Pinkey, wearing a silk wrap, came toward me with her arms outstretched. I stood, though I sat on my impulse to curtsey. She was so elegant. She leaned in, air-kissing me on each cheek, and said, "Delight, how marvelous to see you again! And how advantageous that we'd all wind up in New York City at the same time. You must excuse my appearance, but I'm between fittings and thought I'd come up and see how you're doing. I trust your show is going well."

"Yes, thank you, Mrs. Trueheart-Pinkey. It's going fine."

"Why so formal?" she said, "You can call me Ms. Altovese."

I could actually hear Hailey Joanne rolling her eyes. Ms. Altovese took a seat at the table and asked Mr. Butler the butler to bring her a fruit plate and a cappuccino. Then she turned to us. "What were you two just talking about so intensely?"

Hailey Joanne spoke up. "Mango was just telling me all about her show and . . . um . . . you were about to tell me about, uh . . ."

I figured this was as good a chance as any to tell them about my desperate need for a complete superstar makeover. So, I told them all about Destiny Manaconda singing my song and how she dazzled everyone and how I felt like a plain rice cake next to a chocolate soufflé.

"Oh, Delight, I'm sure you don't have any reason to feel insecure."

"You're a great singer and actor. That's why they wanted you for the part in the first place," Hailey Joanne added.

"Actually, they tried to cast her before me. The only reason she's not in the show is because she's doing Summer Jam concerts all over the country every weekend."

Ms. Altovese reached her bejeweled hand across the table and touched my cheek. "You're beautiful and talented just the way you are."

"Thank you, but the way I am was okay for a middle school show. Now I'm in New York City and I need to change, to be more glamorous. Destiny Manaconda is perfect and that's what I need to be, too."

I watched as Ms. Altovese and Hailey Joanne exchanged glances. Then Hailey Joanne grinned and said, "Well, glamour is our business. If we can't transform you, no one can, am I right, Mother?"

Ms. Altovese's eyes began to sparkle as bright as the diamonds on her fingers. "Of course, we can. And you're in luck. Our glam squad is downstairs waiting to be put to task. Giving you a complete glamorization will be job number one!"

It ain't easy going from basic to goddess. The glam squad worked on me for hours, starting by attaching long clip-in extensions to my hair, which they then cut, curled, and styled. They added individual extensions to my eyelashes, one at a time, gave me a teeth whitening treatment, attached jewel-encrusted fake nails to my hands, and did facial treatments that removed every blackhead and pimple from the surface of Planet Mango. Then they applied layer upon layer of makeup, contouring and reshaping my face until I was almost unrecognizable to myself!

Once the physical transformation was complete, including a designer outfit and heels from Paris that I borrowed, Hailey Joanne and Ms. Altovese began working on my *inner* transformation. I came out of the dressing room wearing the new outfit, thinking I looked amazing. Ms. Altovese asked me to walk across the room. When I did, she and Hailey Joanne gave me a look—the kind you'd have after opening a carton of sour milk.

Hailey Joanne started, "Mango, you can't pull off an outer transformation if you don't change the way you see yourself on the inside."

For the rest of the day, I was critiqued and tutored on how to walk, hold my head high, and enunciate when I spoke. They taught me how to move with the grace of a princess, not just an ordinary girl from around the way. It was hard work being this new kind of me! I realized that Hailey Joanne must have been trained to imagine herself a superstar since before she could walk, and that's why she held herself the way she did, and spoke, walked, and talked the way she did without even thinking about it. I was usually comfortable just being my regular self, but I had to step it up to compete with a star like Destiny Manaconda. I was determined to blow everyone away at the final dress rehearsal tomorrow.

At bedtime, my new clip-in hair was wrapped tightly to my head and covered with a silk bonnet. Hailey Joanne showed me how to sleep on my back with my face pointing up, so as not to ruin my makeup, since the glam squad and Ms. Altovese were leaving early the next morning to do a photo shoot in the Hamptons. It was not easy sleeping so stiff, because normally I sleep on my side, scrunched up in a ball, unconsciously slobbering on my pillow. But somehow I fell asleep, and when I woke up, my makeup was still on, my hair fell around my shoulders in waves, and I could truly relate to my idol, Beyoncé, when she sang, "I woke up like this!"

I pretended I couldn't face2face with my mom because the Wi-Fi in the hotel wasn't very good. I knew she'd have something to say about the brand new me. My mom was more of a down-to-earth type. A little lotion and maybe a smear of lipstick and she was ready to go, which was fine for regular people. But I was about to become a star and I needed to look and act like one.

After a quick breakfast by myself, since Hailey Joanne was still on Paris time, Mr. Versey drove me to the theater for rehearsal. I couldn't wait for the company to get a load of the brand-new, glammed-out me!

CHAPTER TWENTY-NINE

A Certain Quality

M y first stop, when I got to the theater, was the green
room. I wanted TJ and all my friends to see the new
and improved me. When I walked in, they were stretching and
chatting. I had to clear my throat to get their attention. The
expressions on their faces were more startled than amazed.
They all kind of stared at me. TJ said, "Mango? Is that you?"

Using the deeper, more resonant voice I'd been coached to
use, I said, "Of course it's me, silly."

"What happened?" Claxton asked.

"Whatever do you mean?"

Chanté said, "You look so different."

"You even sound different," Chelsea added.

Claxton said, "Did you get a makeover?"

Then LaRon said, "More like a make-*older*. Girl, you look
like you're thirty years old!"

I tried to smile at this remark, but the confidence I felt
when I arrived was beginning to crumble already. Did I look

older instead of better? Had my master plan makeover gone too far?

TJ said, "Hey y'all, chill. Mango is just trying to . . . uh . . . She's trying to . . ." He looked at me. "What *are* you trying to do, Mango?"

My chest felt tight, like I was encased in concrete. I looked around at the faces of my closest friends in the show and felt ridiculous. But I couldn't let them know that. I took a deep breath and repeated what Hailey Joanne had told me: "If you want to be a star, you have to look and act like a star."

Then Larry came into the room and looked around. "Oh, I thought I heard Mango in here," he said, turning to leave.

"I'm Mango."

Larry did a double take and came up close to me. He was about to say something more, but I could tell he stopped himself then said, "Um . . . uh . . . Bob and Roz want to go over the scene with you and your mother, the queen. He's added some new dialogue to make it funnier. Uh . . . yeah."

I followed him onto the stage. The stage lights were on, and it was very warm. Bob had the same double take reaction as Larry when I came onstage. "Uh . . . Mango, is that you under there?"

"Yes, of course it's me!" I was getting a little frustrated with everyone treating me like I was from Mars.

Then Roz came onstage, waving some script pages. "Bobby, Bobby my love. This new material is fantastic, hysterical, and fits my character to a T. Where's Mango? Let's run it a few times."

I took a deep breath. "I'm right here."

Roz squinted at me frowning, then said, "I can't play her mother! I'd have to be in my forties for someone to believe I had a child this old!"

"Excuse me, Roz," Bob said, "but you are in your forties."

"Shut up! I don't look it, do I?"

"Well, no, but . . ."

Roz looked me up and down and leaned in close. "Go wash your face, little girl. You will not age me up in this show."

"Roz . . ." Bob pleaded.

"No! Uh-uh! I didn't sign up for this." She tossed the new script pages onto the floor and stormed offstage.

Bob sighed. "Mango, listen—"

"No. That's not fair!" I realized most of the cast was in the wings, watching me. So, I thought, if Roz could have a hissy fit and storm offstage, so could I!

I held my head high as I headed for the dressing room. Before I reached the stairs, I bumped into Destiny Manaconda coming out of Gabriel Faust's dressing room. I said, "Excuse me."

She looked at me for a moment as if she didn't recognize me. "Mango?"

"Yes?"

"Uh . . . nothing."

I could feel her watching me as I turned and ran up to the third floor as fast as I could, which wasn't that fast at all in heels.

In my dressing room, I looked at myself in the mirror. I was still Mango, wasn't I? But the real Mango, the basic Mango was hidden beneath layers and layers of makeup. I felt like crying, but I stopped myself. I'd spent the whole night trying to sleep on my back like a corpse so I wouldn't ruin my face. Tears would make everything smear, and I wouldn't be able to fix it.

There was a knock at the door, but before I could say anything, it opened and Destiny Manaconda walked in. She looked around the room, which was pretty messy because the Yo, Shady-O crew cared a lot more about having fun than being neat. "I haven't been up here before," she said. "Three flights in six-inch heels is not easy."

I nodded, not sure what to say. This was the first time she had spoken to me since that awful day in the restaurant when she ordered me away from my table. She crossed the room and sat in a chair next to me.

"Why didn't you take the other star dressing room on the first floor? There are two, you know."

"I wanted to be with my friends."

"Oh. I guess I understand that. You and TJ are from the same town and go to school together, right?"

"Yes."

"And the others?"

"I met them here. We like hanging with each other, 'cause we're all around the same age."

"So am I. I'm around the same age as all of you."

It took me a moment, but I realized she was right. She was only three years older than me, but she seemed like an adult, with the way she looked and carried herself. "Yeah, I guess I just think of you as older."

"Price of fame."

"What do you mean?"

"In this business, you have to grow up fast. You're around adults all the time. You kind of forget how to just have fun, you know? When I'm here and I see you and your friends goofing around and giggling and whatnot, I get so jealous."

I gagged. "Jealous of us? What? No way!"

"Seriously!"

"For real? But you and Gabriel Faust, you guys always keep to yourselves."

"That's because it's hard to break out of the bubble after you've been living in one for so long. Real talk, Faustie and I are just friends. The blogs and magazines make so much more of it than what is really going on. We're guilty of making it look like we're a couple, too. Keeps our names in the press, helps sell records. All that breaking up and making up nonsense is good for business."

"But that fight you had at the restaurant?"

"Staged."

"Seriously?"

"Yep. A lot of major bloggers hang out there. The whole thing was online before we walked out."

I was stunned. It all had seemed so real! I was starting to feel some kind of way, because I was ghosted and put in the middle of a fake drama just so they'd be mentioned in gossip blogs. "So . . . Gabriel Faust is *not* your boyfriend?"

"Who has time for a boyfriend? When we're in the same city, we hang around each other a lot because nobody else our age understands what we go through." Something on my dressing table caught her eye. "Are those your Hot Cheetos?" she asked.

"Yeah. You want some?" I handed her the bag.

"Just one." She reached her long nails into the bag, took out a single Cheeto, then placed the bag back on the table.

"How can you eat just one?"

"Listen, if I let myself, I could eat a whole wagonful, but I have to watch my diet. I just look at these things and gain twenty pounds. So I keep my distance, or my manager and agent will throw a fit. I'm telling you, my mouth waters watching you and your friends eating pizza and drinking slushies. My manager makes me weigh in once a week. I get fined if I gain an ounce."

"That's terrible."

"It's what I signed up for. Can't complain now. And that's why I wanted to talk to you."

"Why?"

"Listen, you look good with this whole transformation you did or whatever, but you need to ask yourself, is this really what you want? Because if you fall into the glam trap, it's real hard to get out. That's what happened to me. If I had it to do all over again, I'd take out all of this weave, scrub my face, and just be myself. But my people tell me I have an image to protect, so I can't even leave my house without having my makeup and hair done. It takes hours every day before I can present myself to the world. Is that what you really want?"

I shrugged. "I don't know."

She stood. "Well, think about it. I thought you were fine just the way you were."

"Yeah, but I want to be perfect, like you."

"Perfect? What makes you think I'm perfect?"

"Well, you're successful. You've had TV shows, hit records, modeling . . . that all seems pretty perfect to me."

"That's so funny. I'd give anything if I could spend a week in your shoes. Being able to relax, eat what I want, go where I want without security guards, not be recognized . . . I could just be myself again. That would be a perfect week." She sighed and walked toward the door. "You know, Mango, you have a certain quality that no one else has. Trust it, girl." She waved and left.

A certain quality . . . That's what Bob had said the night he convinced my parents to let me go to New York. But what *was* it? I didn't know. I couldn't figure it out, but maybe that's why I needed to just trust it. I had come this far by being plain old T-shirt, jeans, and Afro puff Mango. Maybe that was enough. Maybe being the best Mango I could be was enough.

I looked at myself in the mirror again, trying to find the regular me underneath all this makeup and hair. It would take a lot of work to look like this every day. Plus, I'd be acting, making believe that I was somebody different from the real me.

Acorn's voice sounded over the intercom. "Half hour to run-through. Half hour!"

Okay . . . so I had thirty minutes to get back to basic— back to me.

CHAPTER THIRTY

A Magic Moment

The final dress rehearsal was in the evening, and it went great. Bob and Larry had let us invite friends and family so we'd get a true feeling of how the show would go over with an audience. And I was feeling good, too. I was back to my real self, without the tons of fake hair and layers of foundation and contour that changed the shape of my face. Even though I had to wear makeup in the show, it was simpler, more natural, and didn't hide who I really was.

The only *awk*-weird thing was the kiss. I had put it off all through rehearsals, and now it was *time to grit my teeth and kiss the creep*. Gabriel and I sang "Duet Forever" (in the lower key, of course), and when we got to the end, things seemed to move in slow motion. We looked into each other's eyes, tilted our heads, and Gabriel went in for the kiss. He took me in his arms, turned my back to the audience, and . . . his lips landed on my chin, directly under my lips. It felt so strange, especially when the audience burst into applause and cheers as though they believed we were really kissing.

The lights went down and we left the stage. "What was that?" I whispered.

"Stage kiss," he said. "I can't go around kissing everyone who wants to kiss me."

Oh really? Yeah, I did practice kissing his poster on the inside door of my closet (a poster I would remove as soon as I got home), and I had thought I wanted to kiss him, but that was before I got to know him. All of the *kissing a creep* anxiety that had built up in me completely vanished. We could *stage kiss* until the end of the run. I was more than perfectly fine with that.

There were a few hiccups during the run through. Nothing serious—a missing prop, a dropped cue. Other than that, the show went well. At the curtain call, Hailey Joanne was on her feet cheering.

Backstage, Hailey Joanne invited the entire Yo, Shady-O crew to come to the Saint Voltaire with us and hang out. She promised that Mr. Versey would drive them all home before it got too late. Everyone immediately whipped out their phones to get permission from their parents or guardians. It wasn't every day you got invited to the fanciest hotel in New York City!

Hailey Joanne was about to call Mr. Butler the butler to ask him to order lots of pizza and snacks for the gang when I had a great idea. "There's this Jamaican bakery in Brooklyn that makes the best food ever! It's owned by my friend, Miss Clover. Maybe you can let her cater the party instead?" Hailey Joanne agreed and relayed the information to Mr. Butler. My mouth watered, thinking of all the great Jamaican food I would eat.

On our way out, we passed the star dressing rooms. Destiny Manaconda was standing by the door, waiting for Gabriel Faust. I walked by, then stopped and walked back to her. I said, "Hi."

"Hi."

"Um, thanks for your advice earlier."

"You're welcome. You were terrific tonight."

My favorite TV star just said I was terrific! I didn't know how to take it or what to say, so I just said, "Thanks." I started to walk away again, but then I turned back. "Hey, a bunch of us are going to the Saint Voltaire to hang out with my friend, Hailey Joanne, in her penthouse. Do you and Gabriel want to come?"

"That sounds fun, but he's gonna be recording songs for his next album tonight."

"What about you?"

She shrugged. "I usually just hang out with him while he records."

"Well, if you feel like coming, we'll be in the penthouse. The one that looks like a castle."

"Okay. We'll see . . ."

I hurried to join Hailey Joanne, TJ, LaRon, Claxton, Chelsea, and Chanté. At the stage door, Bob and Larry warned us not to stay up too late. "Make sure you get your rest! We're opening tomorrow night, and you all need to be in tip-top shape." Mr. Versey assured him that we'd all be nestled in our beds before midnight.

We crammed ourselves into the Pinkeys' SUV. Some of us had to sit in the front and some in the back to fit, and somehow I wound up on TJ's lap. We were all so amped up about the show, talking and laughing nonstop about what went right and what went wrong and how we worked so hard not to crack each other up onstage.

My friends from the show were in awe when we arrived at the penthouse. Hailey Joanne's lifestyle tended to have that effect. Even though I'd already seen the place, I was a little stunned, too—there was a DJ!

I hugged Hailey Joanne and thanked her for being so awesome. "This is nothing," she said. "We've got an even bigger surprise for your opening night."

"What is it? What kind of surprise?"

"Would it be a surprise if I told you?"

"But I want to know now! Tell me, please!"

"Mother would kill me if I did, so forget it." She twirled away from me and grabbed Claxton to dance. I realized she had made a point to sit next to him on the ride over. And now, with the way she was looking at him and touching his arms as they danced, it seemed as though her French crush was a thing of the past.

TJ caught my eye from where he was standing by the DJ booth and started walking toward me, nodding his head and doing some goofy dance moves. I knew he was pretending, because when he was onstage with his band, he moved great. I giggled, and we danced together for so long, I lost track of time. We took a break when the food arrived, though—we were starving! It seemed Mr. Butler had ordered everything on Miss Clover's menu. Everyone loaded up their plates with beef patties, jerk chicken, rice and peas, and carrot cake.

TJ and I went out onto the enormous veranda, carrying our plates piled high with food. New York City looked amazing from up here, sparkling all the way out to the horizon. TJ had kind of a weird smile on his face. He said, "Are you glad you came here this summer?"

"Yeah," I said. "Are you glad you stayed?"

"Yeah." We chewed in silence for a while. I could feel him looking at me, which was awkward, because people really don't look cute biting into a chicken wing.

"What?" I finally said.

"What, what?"

"You keep looking me."

"So?"

"So, I'm eating. It's weird to chew when you're watching me."

He cleared his throat a couple of times and said, "I think you know that I like you. I've always liked you. You're the real reason I stuck around New York. I gave you major attitude that day you went out to lunch with Gabriel Faust because I was jealous. I was afraid you liked him more than me."

"I'm sorry. I didn't mean to make you feel bad, and I don't like him. Not like that."

"But what about me? Do you like me . . . like that?"

My heart was pounding in my chest. I knew I had to be honest—with TJ, and with myself. I took a deep breath. "Yes. I like you . . . like that."

TJ's face lit up with his dazzling smile. I couldn't look away from his kiwi green eyes. We moved toward each other, slowly, shy, and then he leaned in and we kissed. We had kissed many times before, when we played Romeo and Juliet in our school production, but this was different. We weren't pretending to be characters. We were just being ourselves. We weren't acting like we like-liked each other. We actually really did. And this time, for the first time, we didn't have an audience. We were alone. At least, that's what I thought until . . .

"Ahem!"

We leapt apart and turned to see Mr. Versey standing at the entrance to the veranda. "Excuse me, TJ, but it's time for me to escort you back to where you're staying." He smiled with a twinkle in his eye and went back inside.

TJ and I looked at each other and started to laugh. He said, "This just might be the happiest day of my life."

"Mine, too."

After TJ left, I stayed on the veranda, barely noticing the city glittering below like a zillion diamonds. Was TJ my boyfriend now? Did I want a boyfriend? Was I ready for a boyfriend? How would being boyfriend and girlfriend change our friendship?

Suddenly, it seemed like things were happening way too fast. But with the show opening tomorrow, I didn't have time to figure it all out now. I needed to focus—and get a good night's sleep for my big Off-Broadway debut.

CHAPTER THIRTY-ONE

Temper, Temper . . .

Of course, I didn't sleep a wink. I spent the entire night tossing and turning as relentless thoughts crowded my head. It was like my mind was an elevator, stopping at every floor and taking on more passengers with nobody getting off, and each passenger was another worry. *What if the show was a flop? What about TJ? What if I was a flop and the critics blasted me? Were we boyfriend and girlfriend now? What if the show was a hit? Was I old enough to have a boyfriend? What if I was a hit and became a star? Did I even want a boyfriend? Would I wish for my regular life back, like Destiny Manaconda? Would we have to hold hands everywhere we'd go? Would I have to change? Would I be happy? Would we go on dates? Would I have to give up Hot Cheetos and weigh in every week? What did it all mean? What did I really want?*

As the sun was rising, my eyelids began to droop and I finally fell asleep. Luckily, I didn't have to be at the theater until it was time to get ready for the opening night performance. So I slept until the afternoon and probably would have kept on sleeping a few hours more, except Hailey Joanne decided it would be a good idea to shake me awake.

"Come on, wake up! It's time for your surprise."

"No, let me sleep. Please!"

"It's one in the afternoon, you have to get up. Come on, you won't be sorry!"

Groggy and stumbling, I followed her into the living room and saw—MY PARENTS!

"Are you kidding? OMGZ! What are you guys doing here?" I ran to Mom and Dada and crushed them into a group hug. I couldn't believe it. I mean, I had wanted them to come for the show, but Mom kept saying she couldn't take off from work and the travel would be just too expensive.

Dada said, "Ms. Altovese wanted to have a meeting about the catering for her vow-renewal and very kindly suggested we do it here in New York."

Mom added, "And since she was sending her private jet for your father, there was plenty of room for me to come along."

My eyes started to fill with tears of happiness and gratitude, until I remembered—"What about Jasper? Is he all right? Where is he?"

"No need to pop your eyes out," Mom said, laughing. "He's fine. He's at home with Mrs. Kennedy."

I breathed out a dramatic sigh of relief and saw Hailey Joanne and Ms. Altovese watching us from the doorway. I ran over and gave each of them a hug. "Thank you. Thank you so much!"

"You're very welcome, Delight," Ms. Altovese said. "We wanted your opening night to be as spectacular as could be."

"We invited Isabelle too, but . . ." Hailey Joanne trailed off when her mother elbowed her.

I saw Ms. Altovese exchange a look with my parents, and I started to get a bad feeling. "What?" I said. "Will somebody please tell me what's up?"

"Well, we invited her," Mom said, "but she didn't want to come."

"Why not?"

Mom looked at Dada and he said, "She doesn't think you're friends anymore."

I couldn't believe Izzy, my bestie, would pass up a chance to fly to New York to see me in the play! Especially since it would mean getting away from her identity- and crush-stealing cousin Carmella. I had to get to the bottom of this, to find out what was really going on. "I'm going to call her right now."

Mom said, "Okay, Mango, we'll be here."

As soon as I got to my room, I face2faced Izzy, but she didn't pick up. I tried just regular calling and got voicemail, so I texted:

M   Izzy?

M   Why didn't you come to New York 2 see the show?
What's going on?

The little dots didn't start pulsing. Was she busy? Or maybe her phone was off? I wracked my brain, trying to figure out what she could be doing . . . and then I realized that I hadn't spoken to her in, well, almost a week. I had been so busy with run-throughs and tech rehearsals, for adding the lights, sound, costumes, and set changes to the production. There were some nights I didn't leave the theater until one in the morning. If anybody would understand how hectic tech week could be, Izzy would. . . . Wouldn't she?

There was a knock at the door, and Hailey Joanne popped her head in.

"What did Izzy say?" she asked, coming to sit beside me on the bed.

"Nothing! I tried everything, but she hasn't answered my calls *or* my texts. Maybe she's out and she left her phone at home?"

"Have you ever known Izzy to move five feet without her phone?"

"No." Izzy broke out in a cold sweat if her phone wasn't in reaching distance.

Hailey Joanne held up her phone. "You want me to find out what's up?" I nodded, and Hailey Joanne face2faced Izzy, motioning for me to keep quiet.

I almost couldn't believe it when Izzy picked up immediately. "Hailey Joanne?"

"Hi. I was just calling to see if you were okay. You know, since you didn't come to New York and all."

"Did Mango ask you to call?"

"No. Why?"

"Come on, Hailey Joanne, it's not like we're close enough for you to face2face me."

"Okay, look, Mango is really upset that you're not coming to see the show. She's wondering why."

"Tell her to check her phone log. Maybe then she'll understand why."

I knew it. She was mad because I hadn't talked to her for about a week. How petty could she be? Hailey Joanne gave a slight shake of her head to keep me from talking.

"She's been really busy with the show, you know."

"Well I think the show has gone to her head. Now that she's a star in New York, she's too good to talk to her friends or at least the people she used to consider her friends."

I couldn't hold it in any longer. I grabbed Hailey Joanne's phone, "How dare you say that about me! I haven't changed at all!"

"Yes, you have. You only think about yourself. Every time we talk, you jump right into what's happening in your exciting Off-Broadway life and then it's 'Oh, by the way, what's up with you?' I'm always an afterthought."

"I thought you wanted to know what was going on in New York. I was sharing what was happening to me to make you forget about how sick you were of your miserable cousin!"

"Don't call my cousin miserable!"

"You're the one who says you can't stand her!"

"Only *I* can say that she's my miserable cousin!"

"Great! Well, I hope you two will be miserable ever after together."

"She already went back to Texas! Which you would have known if you answered any of my calls!"

"Then you can be miserable by yourself!" I ended the call and tossed Hailey Joanne's phone on the bed. "I don't care if I ever speak to her or see her again," I declared.

"Mango . . ."

"I mean it! You know what, she's just jealous. She thinks she should be here in New York because she thinks she's the greatest star who ever lived. I was trying really hard to include her and make her feel like she was a part of everything, and then she goes and accuses me of being selfish and having a big head!"

"Mango, you need to calm down. Your show is opening tonight."

"That's another thing, she *would* pick today of all days to show her true colors. I would have been so happy if she'd come to see the show. I never meant to make her feel bad." My face was hot. My eyes filled with tears. I lay down, turning my face away from Hailey Joanne. "Will you tell my parents I'm gonna shower, and then I'll be down for lunch?"

"Sure," she said. "Sorry. I never should have called her."

"Don't be sorry. It's not your fault."

When I heard the door close after Hailey Joanne left the room, I couldn't help myself. I broke down and cried. Losing a best friend was something I should have been used to by now, but it really hurt. It hurt just as bad as it did before.

—

I felt strangely out of sync as the rest of the day went by, like when you watch a movie and the actors' mouths are moving but the dialogue is a beat behind. I couldn't get Izzy out of my mind. I was so angry with her! I kept making up arguments in my head to convince myself that it was all her fault and I should be glad she wouldn't be a part of my life anymore.

Aunt Zendaya came to the Saint Voltaire to join Mom, Dada, and me for lunch, but even though the food was delicious and I was happy to be surrounded by my family, I had to force myself to stay present and pay attention. After we ate, Dada actually did have a meeting with Ms. Altovese to go over the menu for her vow-renewal ceremony. Mom and Aunt Zendaya decided to visit their old neighborhood, go shopping, and stop by my favorite Jamaican bakery so Mom could, in her words, "hug Miss Clover's neck and give her a pair of tickets to the show." I thought about going with them—maybe a plantain tart would make me feel better? But I decided not to, telling them I needed to rest up for opening night.

Mango in the City

As I headed back to my room, I must have looked some kind of way because Hailey Joanne offered to cancel the plans she'd made to hang out with Claxton. I assured her I would be fine. I wanted to be alone and I had lots of lost sleep to make up for anyway if I was going to be ready for tonight's performance.

CHAPTER THIRTY-TWO

Yellow Roses

Backstage on opening night, everyone and everything was buzzing with excitement. The "company of parrots" had obviously been chattering, because as soon as I arrived, Bob called me into his office. He was wearing black cargo shorts and a T-shirt with a tuxedo print on it. He offered me a seat and sat down across from me.

"I heard about the fight with Izzy."

"How?"

"Well, Hailey Joanne told someone and he told someone and so on and so on until TJ told me. He's a little worried about you, and so am I. I know you girls are close."

"*Were* close. We were besties. At least, that's what I thought."

Bob nodded sympathetically. "How're you holding up?"

"I don't know," I admitted. "I was so angry before, but now I just feel numb . . . and maybe a little distracted."

"When I'm feeling distracted or numb, it's usually because I'm trying to avoid feeling the feelings I should be feeling. I don't want to admit when I'm afraid or nervous or sad or hurt. So I retreat to a place inside myself where I don't feel anything. But what do I always say when you get confused or worried about how to play a scene?"

I thought back to the first time we did *Yo, Romeo!* back when I was insecure so much of the time. "Start from where you are?"

"That's right. Start from where you are. Your character is feeling exactly what you're feeling."

"But right now, I'm feeling nothing."

"That's what you think, but really, deep down, you're feeling a lot. Right?"

My throat started to tighten, and my breath started coming in gulps. I was trying to keep the tears from spilling over. Bob took my hand and said, "Let it out, Mango. Let it all go."

I cried. Not just an ordinary cry, but a big, gulping kind of cry with giant tears streaking my face and snot running from my nose. Bob came from behind his desk and held me as I sobbed into his shoulder. It was a good five minutes before I pulled myself together and realized I was wiping my nose on his tuxedo T-shirt.

"Sorry."

"It's A-okay. It's 'snot' a real tux anyway."

Despite everything, I had to giggle at his corny joke.

"Now that you've got your feelings working again," Bob said, "use them. You are Juliet, and Juliet is you. Start where you are and let the character and the play take you where you need to go."

"I will," I said, standing up.

"I'll have the crew move your costumes and things downstairs to the second star dressing room, just for tonight. Is that all right? I think your feelings might still be a little tender to be hanging with the gang."

"Yes, thank you."

"And I'll dig up an ice pack. So you don't have to make your Off-Broadway debut with puffy eyes."

⸻

"Five minutes. Five minutes to places!" Acorn's voice rang out from the second star dressing room's intercom.

"Thank you, five!" I called, even though I knew he couldn't hear me. I looked at myself in the mirror. The ice pack had de-puffed my eyes, my hair and makeup were done, and my costume completed my look. I was Juliet. I was still feeling a bit fragile but I was ready to go. There was a soft knock at the door. "Come in."

TJ stepped into the room, his hands behind his back. "You okay?"

"Yeah, I'm fine."

"Bob told the company to give you space tonight, so I guess I'm sort of breaking the rules."

"I'm glad you did." After the big fight with Izzy this morning, I had almost forgotten about TJ, what he had told me last night, the kiss . . . Looking into his kiwi green eyes now, I felt heat rising to my cheeks and I had to look away.

TJ cleared his throat. "I hope I didn't weird you out with the stuff I said last night."

"No, you didn't . . . but . . . yeah, you kinda did."

"Sorry."

Just then, Acorn's voice sounded over the intercom again. "Places. Places for the top of act one."

"Thank you, places!" TJ and I said simultaneously, and then we both burst into laughs.

"Can we talk more later?" I asked.

"Yeah, I'd like that," TJ said. "I'm supposed to be on stage left, so I'd better scram." As he turned to leave, I saw he was holding a vase with yellow roses behind his back.

"Nice flowers," I said.

He turned back, blushing. "Oh! These are for you! Happy opening!" He handed me the vase.

"Thank you. They're beautiful," I said, blushing even harder.

"For hundreds of years, yellow roses have been a way to tell someone how much joy they bring to your life and how much you appreciate their friendship."

The intercom speaker crackled a third time. "Places, people!"

TJ jumped. "Gotta go!"

"Break legs!" I called.

I lifted the flowers to my nose and took a whiff. No boy

had ever given me roses before. It made feel special. After setting them in the center of my dressing table, I finally left my dressing room and headed for stage right, where I'd make my first entrance. It was time. My parents, my aunt, and my friends were in the audience, and I was ready to give them my best performance ever.

CHAPTER THIRTY-THREE

A Lot to Learn

Opening night. Off-Broadway, in New York City! What could be more exciting? I was in my first professional production. I was one of the stars of a show that could go all the way to Broadway! It should have been the highlight of my summer, but then the curtain parted and Gabriel Faust swaggered onstage and nothing went as I expected.

The actual show went pretty well, I guess. At least the parts of it I could hear. The thing was, whenever Gabriel Faust appeared onstage or sang a song, about fifty girls in the audience screamed their throats out. Fifty girls, in a theater with only ninety-nine seats! It was so weird. When he made his first entrance and the screams started, I thought the set must be falling or that something else catastrophic was happening. But it was just him. These "Faustnatics" were relentless! The only time they calmed down was when he wasn't onstage. Then the energy level in the theater plummeted—until he returned. At least that was how it felt to me.

During the curtain call, the Faustnatics rushed the stage, tossing flowers and gifts to their idol. He winked and blew kisses at them, reveling in the sensation he was causing. It was a little weird for the rest of us, but at least we would probably sell out the entire run if Gabriel and his Faustnatics kept this up.

When I got back to my dressing room, I was so tired, I didn't even close the door and just plopped down on my chair without removing the silver sequined gown I wore in the final scene. I heard a knock, and then Bob poked his head in. "Mango, you were magnificent!" he gushed.

"I was?" I couldn't be sure, with all the fan-demonium over Gabriel. I didn't think anyone could hear the dialogue or the songs.

"Are you kidding? You had half the audience in tears when Juliet died."

I sighed. "They were probably crying for Gabriel Faust."

"Listen, don't fall for that stunt."

"Stunt?"

"I'll just say this, and if you tell anyone, I'll deny deny deny. Frances Francisco, the manager to the stars, demanded a block of fifty tickets and, well . . . let's just say she tilted the scales in her client's favor."

My jaw dropped. "For real?"

"Oh, my sweet, innocent Mango. You have a lot to learn."

"Mango!" A bunch of voices called my name, and when I looked to the door of my dressing room, all of a sudden, there were so many people! Mom, Dada, Aunt Zendaya, Hailey Joanne, Ms. Altovese, TJ, and the Yo, Shady-O crew all piled in, congratulating me and showering me with hugs and kisses. Surrounded by all these people I cared about, I started to feel like maybe I did pretty okay after all.

—

The cast party was held onstage. It was pretty low-key, especially compared to the party we'd had at Hailey Joanne's the night before. Gabriel Faust never really joined us, except for the toast from Bob, Larry, and the producers. Afterward, Frances Francisco escorted her client to the stage door, where he signed autographs and posed for selfies with his fans. Then he and Destiny Manaconda were whisked away in his luxury SUV.

With Gabriel gone for the night, everyone seemed to let out a breath and relax. TJ was in the pit, jamming with the band. Aunt Zendaya and Acorn were sitting very close to each other on the stairs leading up to the dressing rooms, talking and laughing. Hailey Joanne and Claxton were dancing on the stage. Chelsea, Chanté, and LaRon were all busy entertaining their boyfriends, so I was kind of by myself. But that was fine. I wasn't in much of a party mood anyway.

Walking back to my dressing room, I was intercepted by Zippy. Ever since she accused me of lying and quit being my escort, we hadn't had much to do with each other outside of our shared scenes. So I was surprised when she grabbed my arm and told me, "Hey, kiddo, you were surprisingly good out there tonight."

"Uh . . . thanks."

"I was laying bets you'd choke. I mean, with all your best friend drama and this being your first time in a real show and all, I figured you'd go down in flames. But on the contrary, you came through. Good for you."

I was astonished. "Did you actually place bets?"

"I wanted to, but none of the others wanted to play along. They thought it might jinx the show. There were a bunch of theater bloggers in the audience and the rest of the chumps didn't want to risk it."

"Theater bloggers?"

"Yeah! Who do you think reviews these Off-Off-Off Broadway showcases? If they rave, big time producers, agents, and managers will come sniffing around. If they give us the old thumbs down, you'll have to hire private jets to get any of the muckety-mucks to journey below Fourteenth Street."

"How do *you* think it went?" I asked.

"We'll soon find out," Zippy said, shrugging. "I know I got my laughs, though, so I'll probably get noticed. Maybe I won't have to give up my tap shoes and become a civilian after all. Toodles!"

As she wandered off, my fingernails started to tingle the way they always did when I wanted to bite them. Now I was worrying about the theater bloggers. I was so glad I hadn't known they were in the audience while I was still onstage. That would have really made me nervous, and that was not the kind of emotion that would have been good for my character.

When I got to my dressing room, the door was slightly ajar and I was surprised to hear people talking. I paused to listen. "Listen, Mr. and Mrs. Fuller . . . it is Fuller, right?" It was Frances Francisco talking to my parents.

Dada said, "Last time I checked, yes."

"Great. You're so handsome. Could have been onstage yourself. Seriously!"

Mom said, "Are you flirting with my husband?"

Frances Francisco snorted. "If I were, my wife would kill me!"

Dada laughed good-naturedly, but Mom's chuckle didn't have a drop of amusement in it.

"So your girl, Mango, she's got it. You know? The *it* factor. I kid you not. I can spot talent, but talent is not enough. You've got to have that light, that sparkle that makes you stand out among the rest. This entire cast is talented, but Mango, and Faustie of course, they're the only ones who truly shine. She's got a bright future ahead of her, and I want to be her guide."

Someone came up behind me and tapped me on the shoulder. I gasped. It was TJ. I guess Frances Francisco heard me, because she peered out of the door and said, "The adults are having a serious discussion, right now. Go have fun." And she closed the door to *my* dressing room!

I was a little stunned and embarrassed that I'd been caught eavesdropping. TJ laughed and said, "Can we have that talk now?"

I said, "Yeah, I guess this is the time for *serious discussions.*"

He took my hand and led me out of the theater.

CHAPTER THIRTY-FOUR

The Kindness of Bloggers

We sat next to each other on the steps to the stage door. There was a gentle breeze that reminded me of nights sitting outside back at home, but the scent was pure New York—a mixture of Chinese takeout, fried chicken, car exhaust, and urine. The sounds of the band playing back in the theater mingled with the breeze.

"I thought you'd be jamming with the band all night long," I said.

"Yeah. It's been a while since I've been in touch with the musician side of me. Maybe I should have been in the pit all along. It was fun playing with professionals."

"You're just as professional as they are."

"But I don't make a living doing it," TJ said. "They do."

"You're not out of school yet. And I bet none of them is as good a songwriter as you are."

He turned away, smiling shyly. Then he leaned over and bumped me with his shoulder. "You're good for my ego."

"I'm just being honest." I looked at TJ, and he looked back

at me. As I gazed into his green eyes, he leaned in slowly . . . and I wasn't sure why I did it, but at the last second, I turned my head. His lips landed on my cheek.

"Whoa. Sorry," he said.

"I don't know why I did that. I'm . . ." I trailed off.

"It's okay. Are you . . . is it that you're not ready to have a boyfriend yet?"

"I'm not sure. I mean, I like you, a lot. A really lot. But . . . if I was ready, would I be wondering if I was ready? We're friends, too. Good friends. What if this ruins our friendship?"

"Yeah, I worry about that, too. That's why it took me weeks to tell you how I felt."

"So . . . what should we do?"

"I guess we could stay friends. Or . . ." It was TJ's turn to trail off.

He looked off into the night, with a pondering look on his face. I held my breath waiting for him to go on. Finally, I punched him in the thigh and said, "Or WHAT???"

He laughed and rubbed his thigh, "You're so cute when you take your impatience out on my leg."

"Ha ha! Go on and finish what you were saying."

"I was trying to put it into words. I'm a songwriter, right? I've got to find the right words."

As he struggled for the right words, I realized that I knew what needed to be said, so I nudged him with my shoulder. "Listen TJ, we both know how we feel about each other and that's good, but maybe we should just take it slow."

"What do you mean by that?"

"It just means we're special to each other and we treat each other that way and give things a chance to develop . . . until we're sure of what we want to call our relationship. We can hang out. Go to the movies."

"Your parents let you date?"

"No way! We can go in a group. We'll sit together and share popcorn."

"Who's buying?"

"We'll take turns."

TJ laughed. "Good answer!" He held out his palm. "Can we hold hands at the movies?" I took his hand. "Yeah. I guess that's slow."

"You can invite me over for dinner, so your parents can get to know me."

"And you can invite me to dinner at your house."

"Yeah, but my parents split up a long time ago. My dad lives in L.A. And my mom is about to remarry, and it's kind of freaking me out."

"Oh. I didn't know any of that."

"I don't talk about it much. I either squash it or put it in songs."

"You can talk to me," I offered.

"Yeah. I know," TJ said, smiling. "That's a part of what makes you special to me."

Was I ready to have a boyfriend? Maybe not . . . but I was maybe ready to see where things could go with TJ. I leaned in and kissed him on the cheek. We sat there for a few minutes, holding hands, not needing to say anything.

Our comfortable silence was interrupted when the stage door suddenly banged open. TJ and I scrambled out of the way before we were run over by Frances Francisco. She was shouting into her headset. "Bring the car around. Now!"

TJ and I looked at each other. The music from the band jamming and all the laughter and chatter from the party had stopped. Something was up. We hurried inside to find out what it was.

—

Onstage, everyone was crowded around Zippy as she read from her phone. "The songs were cute, but unmemorable. The book was perfect . . . for a school play. The squealing girls in the audience were a testament to that. The object of their idolatry, Gabriel Faust, played Romeo with the depth of a piece of wet cardboard and his singing . . . well, luckily his thin voice and flat notes were mostly drowned out by the squealing of his rabid fans. The one bright spot in the show was his Juliet. Mango Delight Fuller, a genuine middle school kid with a cool name, is believable, relatable, and charismatic, and she sings like a dream. Too bad there isn't more of her and much less of him! Walk, don't run to catch this one."

An audible groan went up. Zippy turned to Bob, whose whole essence seemed to be drooping. "Sorry, bro. Better luck next time."

He asked, "Is that the only one? The only review?"

"Nope, but it's the kindest." She turned and pointed to me. "The kiddo over there is the only one who came out smelling like a rose . . . or should I say, a mango? They all gushed over her."

Everyone looked at me. My mouth opened and closed. I wasn't sure how to respond, especially to their weak smiles and vague nods.

But then my Yo, Shady-O crew came over, giving me hugs and high fives. Hailey Joanne was there, too. She squeezed my hand and whispered in my ear, "Don't you dare make yourself feel bad about being so good."

Dada grabbed me in a hug. "My heart is poppin' outta me chest. I'm so proud of you!"

"I'm proud of you too, sweetheart." Mom moved Dada out of the way so she could embrace me. All this love was the best feeling in the world. When Mom let go, I saw everyone was picking up their things and heading out. I guessed the party was over. "Let's find Mr. Versey and head back to the hotel," Mom said. "Dada and I have an early flight."

As we were leaving the theater, TJ gave me a quick hug. "I'll call you later," he said, and then he winked at me. Winked? Was that a part of the *taking it slow* thing? We've got to wink at each other? If that was the case, I was in trouble. I'd always had a problem winking. Either both my eyes closed or both of them stayed open, so it looked like I was blinking. I had even tried holding one eye open with my finger while closing the other, to build up my winking muscles, but it didn't work, so I gave up. I'd accepted the fact that I'd be un-wink-able for life.

I was so deep in thought on the ride uptown, I almost didn't notice someone was missing. "Where's Aunt Zendaya?"

"She left with Popcorn," Mom said.

Huh? Oh! "Mom! You mean Acorn!"

"Oh, right. I knew it was some kind of corn."

Well, that broke the ice and we all burst out laughing. It had been a day with lots of ups and downs and this was the perfect way to end it.

CHAPTER THIRTY-FIVE

A Farewell to the Parents

M om and Dada were flying back at six in the morning, because Mom had to show up for work at Target and they didn't want to be away from Jasper too long. I got up at four to go to the airport with them. Of course, Mr. Versey was there right on time ready to drive us, looking as crisp as a fresh head of lettuce.

When we were on our way, Mom brought up a subject I had avoided the night before. "So, Mango, that woman, Ms. Francisco, she had a talk with us last night."

"I know and my answer is, no. No way."

"How can you have answer when you don't even know the question?"

I knew the question. "She wants to manage me, right?"

"Yes."

Dada stretched and yawned. "So . . . why so emphatic with the negative response? Don't you like her?"

"Nope."

"Why not?"

I took a deep breath. "She made me lie about why Gabriel Faust wasn't at rehearsal after he ghosted me at lunch. And she's really bossy and tricky and . . . I don't know . . . her hands are huge!"

Dada's eyebrows lifted. "What the size of her hands got to do with anything?"

I shrugged. "I don't know . . ."

"I never even noticed her hands."

"I did!" Mom said. "Her fingers looked like a a great big bunch of ripe plantains."

Dada shook his head. "Oh come on, Margie. The woman was nice."

"You're just saying that because *the woman* said you were cute. Please. She was just trying to get in your head so she could manipulate you. You know what they say, flattery will get you when the truth won't."

"Flattery? Truth? You trying to say I not cute?"

Mom folded her arms across her chest defiantly, "Cute or not, I don't trust her, and Mango doesn't want to work with her, so that's that."

"But the woman said Mango could make enough money to pay for college *and* graduate school in just a few years if she got the right job. Why not take the chance, as long as Mango enjoys what she's doing?"

"I agree," Mom said. "But if this woman can see how talented Mango is, other agents and managers will be able to see it, too. She's not the only bean in the stew." Mom turned away from Dada and looked at me. "Mango, if you met another agent or manager that you liked, would you want to continue performing?"

"Yes, of course. But I could also go back to school and get scholarships for college or something later on."

Mom put a hand on mine. "But you absolutely don't want to work with this San Francisco woman, right?"

I felt uncomfortable choosing when Mom and Dada were on opposite sides of anything, but I really didn't want to be managed by—"*Frances* Francisco, Mom, not *San* Francisco. And no. I don't want to work with her. She makes me very uncomfortable."

Mom slapped her hands on her thighs triumphantly. "All right then, 'nuff said."

Dada shrugged, crossed his legs in the opposite direction from Mom, folded his arms across his chest and looked out the window. Mom smiled at me, shook her head, and winked. (What was with winking all of a sudden?)

She slid closer to Dada. "And listen here, Mr. Man. There is only one woman you need to worry about thinking you're cute, and that's me! You're *my* husband. I think you're cute and that's that, 'nuff said."

Dada, still looking out the window, smiled, unfolded his arms, and reached a hand to Mom. She put her hand in his and he pulled her close. The argument was over and *erry-ting was irie once more.* No worries. One love. Peace. 'Nuff said!

The ride back to the hotel was quiet. Saying goodbye to my parents brought back the feeling of homesickness I thought I'd left behind weeks ago. Since Hailey Joanne and Ms. Altovese were checking out of the Saint Voltaire in the afternoon, I was planning on sleeping for a few more hours, packing my things, and then heading to Aunt Zendaya's apartment before doing the show that night. But you know what they say about the best laid plans? They made the universe ROFL that you thought things would work out smoothly.

Back at the hotel, snuggled in the gigantic, fluffy, king-size bed, I was this close to falling asleep when my phone buzzed. I was going to ignore it, until I realized it might be my parents calling from the airport. Maybe their flight was canceled. Maybe they decided to stay another day. Or . . . maybe they missed their flight!!!

Or . . .

Maybe it was Izzy.

I looked at the caller ID on my phone. It was from Acorn. I had better pick up.

"We're calling everyone into the theater this morning at ten for rehearsal," he said.

My mouth dropped open. "Rehearsal? What for? Was the show that bad last night?"

"I can't say over the phone. You'll find out when you get here. Do you have a ride?"

"Yes, I'm sure Mr. Versey will drop me off."

"Perfect. See you at ten," he said, hanging up. What the heck was going on???

CHAPTER THIRTY-SIX

Bitter and Sweet

The rest of the cast was assembled in the audience when I got to the theater, waiting to find out what was up. Most of us were grumpy at being called so unexpectedly and some were hungover and in pain. Why were we being called so early on a show day? Now that our first show was over, we only had to be at the theater a half hour before curtain—unless something catastrophic happened overnight.

TJ arrived and sat next to me, taking my hand in his and squeezing it. He looked nervous and agitated—*agit-ervous*. I asked, "Do you know what's going on?"

He started to shake his head no, then changed his mind and nodded yes. "I do, but I can't say anything."

"Why not?"

"I just can't. You'll find out in a minute."

He squeezed my hand tighter. I guess he needed someone to hold onto and I wanted to be there for him.

Bob and Larry entered and crossed to center stage. The theater went silent. Bob's eyes were bloodshot and he looked pale, which was impressive since he'd been getting more and more tan as the summer went on. Larry paced back and forth, his lips a tight line of tension.

Bob took a deep breath and began. "Um . . . Gabriel Faust is no longer in the show."

The room exploded with gasps. "What! Since when?" I heard Zippy shout. "You're kidding! OMG!"

Bob held his hand up for silence. "We've been informed by his manager, Frances Francisco"—he said her name through clenched teeth—"that her client has suddenly come down with a case of chicken pox—"

Larry butted in. "But we all know that's chicken poop!"

"Larry, please. She texted a photo of what looked like some kind of rash to me."

Larry snarled, "Yeah, savage reviews can cause one to break out."

"Stop it, Larry."

Zippy stood up and thrust her fist into the air. "Larry is right. This is outrageous. You should sue the jerk!" Her demand was met with a chorus of angry agreement.

"We're having our lawyers look into it, but lawsuits take time," Bob said. "And we're only running a couple of weeks. We've got to move forward. So we are going to continue the show with TJ taking on the role of Romeo."

There was a gasp. The room went silent. I looked at TJ, but he wouldn't look at me or anyone. No wonder he was so *agit-ervous*. He was being thrust back into the lead role just as abruptly as he had been tossed out! I felt bad and glad for him at the same time. Bad because he was under a lot of pressure right now. But glad because I knew he'd be perfect as Romeo and this was the entire reason he'd come to New York in the first place. "Don't worry," I told him, squeezing his hand. "You're going to be great!"

After a long day of rehearsing and costume alterations, since TJ was taller and more muscular than Gabriel Faust, it was showtime. About a third of the audience had asked for refunds once they found out the star was gone and his understudy would be stepping in. But that still left us with about sixty people—and the show was amazing! We got a standing ovation that was meant for the entire cast, not just one diva celebrity. When TJ stepped forward to take his bow, the entire company cheered and applauded along with the audience.

Even though the show kept getting better and better with TJ as Romeo, the audiences got smaller and smaller. When we arrived at the theater for the last performance of our first week, a Closing Notice was posted on the call board— effective immediately after the matinee.

It looked like I was going home a week earlier than planned. Even though my parents' visit had reawakened my homesickness, now I didn't want to leave. The entire company, onstage and backstage, had grown so close. All the drama with Gabriel Faust had bonded us and we wanted to stick it out. But Bob and Larry told us it just wasn't financially possible. Without Gabriel, the backers refused to put in the money that could tide us over through the next week.

People started throwing out ideas, offering to cut our pay or take no pay at all, anything to save the show. But it was no use. We were closing—no ifs, ands, or buttocks.

Acorn called Aunt Zendaya with the news, so she could meet us at the theater after the matinee. Then we played and sang our hearts out for the twenty people in the audience, and when all twenty of them were standing, cheering, and stomping their feet during the curtain call, we felt vindicated. We came, we saw, we slayed!

———

That evening, while I was packing my suitcase and Acorn and Aunt Z were in the kitchen preparing something that smelled so good, it was making my mouth water, my face2face ringtone went off.

It was Izzy. I picked up.

"Mango . . ." she started.

"Izzy . . ."

"I'm sorry the show is closing."

"How did you find out?"

"Theater blogs, of course. I wanted to call you to make

sure you weren't feeling too bad . . . and to apologize. I'm so sorry about the way I acted. I should have come to New York to see the show. I wanted to . . . but I was so jealous! Of you and of Carmella being with Hector Osario. I was so jealous, my eyes were crossed. It's taken me a week of having arguments with you and myself in my mind. I'm sorry. I read your reviews and everyone loves you. So do I."

"Thanks, Iz. I'm sorry, too! Maybe my head *was* getting too big. I mean, I should have found time to at least let you know I was too busy to talk. A bestie deserves that much consideration. Especially since I knew you were having a rough time. I'm going to be more considerate, I swear."

"I felt horrible, too. But I hope we can put it behind us so we can both feel better?"

"Talking to you is making me feel better already. I missed you, girl. And I'm so glad we're making up, because guess what?"

"What?"

"I'll be home tomorrow!"

"Yes! You have to spend the night at my house. Girrrrrl, I have so much to tell you!"

"What-what? Tell me now."

"No way!"

"Please! My impatience runneth over!"

"Okay, so . . . you know about Hector Osario and Carmella?"

"Yeah . . ."

"Well, my double-crossing, bodysnatching cousin took me

with her to a dinner at Hector's house, and I met his cousin, Raymond Rivera. OMGZ! He's ten times cuter than Hector *and* he plays guitar!"

"Get out!"

"Get in! And guess what?"

"Don't make me guess, I'm dying!"

"He's writing a song for me! He played the melody for me over the phone last night."

"And . . .?"

"Tune in tomorrow. If you wanna know the juicy details, you'd better get your butt over here as soon as your flight lands."

"Okay, but I've got to go home and squeeze my baby brother first. Then I'm on my way. Besides, girl, you're not the only one with juice to spill."

"I'm so sure! I can't wait to hear all about you and Gabriel Faust and Destiny Manaconda—"

"And TJ."

"What?"

"Mm-hmm!"

"OMGZ, this is epic!"

We went on and on talking and laughing for hours. We only stopped for about a half hour while I had dinner. Aunt Z and Acorn outdid themselves with their vegan version of a Vietnamese vermicelli dish called bún. It was amazing! Just before I went to bed, as I was plugging in my phone, I realized I had a voicemail from a number I didn't recognize.

Who left voicemails nowadays? Texting was so much easier. I bent down to where my phone was plugged in and listened to the message.

"Hi Mango, it's Destiny . . . Manaconda? Listen, I told my manager about you and he saw the matinee today and wants to meet you. Do you think you can stick around for a few days? You have my number now, so let me know what to tell him."

I sat stone-still on the floor for a few minutes, just holding my phone. What did this mean? Did I really want to stick around to meet a manager that might want me to weigh in weekly and swear off Hot Cheetos?

My phone buzzed. It was a text from TJ.

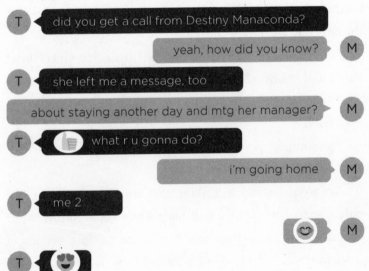

CHAPTER THIRTY-SEVEN

Here We Go Again?

Mom and Dada picked me up from the airport. When we got back to our apartment, I squeezed and hugged my little brother, quickly unpacked, and ran to Izzy's house to spend the night. We had so much fun, we decided to make it a once-a-week date. It was the perfect welcome home, and with school starting soon, I was looking forward to getting back into a routine.

But that was before I realized that once again, things were going to change . . .

Maxwell Paige, Destiny Manaconda's manager, had contacted Mom and Dada, saying it was urgent he meet us. He flew out the next day and took us to lunch along with TJ and his mother. We went to The Grainery, a super fancy macrobiotic restaurant. Actually, I had been hoping for a cheeseburger and fries, but to be honest, the food was DOPE!

Mr. Paige was really nice. In fact, he was actually pretty cool. He was tall and slim and wore a pinstripe suit that was obviously tailor-made. He looked like Jay-Z, but a little older and with a shaved head. It didn't take long for him to cut to the chase.

"Mr. and Mrs. Fuller, Ms. Gatt, Mango, TJ— I caught the final performance of *Yo, Romeo!* Mango and TJ, you're very talented, and I'd like to manage both of you. You know that I work with Destiny Manaconda, and from my website and the other info I emailed, you'll see I only work with the very best. That's you two."

Dada spoke up. "We did check out your website and we were very impressed, but Mango has to decide for herself." Everyone turned to me. "What do you think?"

I looked at Mr. Paige and said, "Hot Cheetos."

He said, "I beg your pardon?"

"Hot Cheetos. I won't give them up. Destiny Manaconda says she can't eat them and that you make her weigh in every week."

Mr. Paige chuckled. "You won't have to give up your snack. Destiny is under contract as a spokeswoman and model for the Dalvin Couture Collection. It is they who insist she weigh in each week to make sure she stays camera ready. I'll admit it is tough for her, but her healthy bank account and the latest designer fashions make it all worthwhile."

"Oh. Well . . . I need some time to think about it."

"Yeah, me too," TJ added.

"Unfortunately, we don't have a lot of time. You see, the

reason I flew here to meet you is because Destiny's been cast in a new series. I'm not allowed to give many details at this point, but it's about a teen garage band that hits it big. You two would be perfect as her bandmates, and Destiny wants you in the show. I think you're both terrific, and I'm positive the network will go wild for you." He paused to take a sip of water. "Here's the thing, we would need you on the West Coast in two days for a screen test. We start shooting the pilot next week. If you're interested, I'll have to know before we leave the restaurant."

My stomach dropped. I looked at my parents. Mom's mouth was agape. Dada was grinning from ear to ear. How on earth was I going to figure this out before the end of lunch? My head was spinning!

TJ cleared his throat. "Can Mango and I talk in private for a couple of minutes?"

We excused ourselves from the table and stepped outside. "What do you think?" he asked.

"I don't know . . ." I said. "This is amazing, but we just got back, and school starts in two weeks. I like being at home with my friends, you know?"

"Can I be honest?"

"No, lie to me. Dishonesty is the best policy!"

"Okay, okay," TJ laughed. "Listen, I told you my mother is getting married and all. Anyway, I've been kind of feeling like a third wheel around my house with all the wedding stuff.

Getting back a week early threw a wrench in my mother's plans."

"Oh."

"And . . . my dad lives out in L.A. I hardly ever get to see him. This would give us a chance to hang, and who knows what could happen from there?"

"So, you want to go?"

"Not without you."

Everything was happening so fast. I was feeling like a yo-yo again, spinning up and down and all around. I had just gotten home, back to my family and friends and all the little comforts I had missed when I was in New York. Did I really want to go to a strange place with strange people all over again, so soon? Then I remembered what Acorn had said when he had escorted me back to Aunt Zendaya's place the first time: "Embrace the fact that things are going to be uncomfortable for a while, but one day soon, things will start falling into place and you'll start to fit in . . . until the next time you step out of your comfort zone."

He was right. At first, being in the show in New York was uncomfortable. Then things got better, and I got so comfortable that I didn't want to leave. Maybe this was that *next time* he was talking about.

I'd never been in a TV show before. It was probably a lot different from working on a play. What would it be like in Hollywood, being in a studio with cameras? I started getting excited imagining being on screens all over the country, and maybe the world! I would be bananas to pass on a new experience like this.

I looked at TJ, and he looked at me. The sparkle in my eyes ignited a spark in his. I grabbed his hand, and we walked back into the restaurant. We had decided. Hollywood, here we come!

Mango Delight Fuller
is headed to Hollywood!

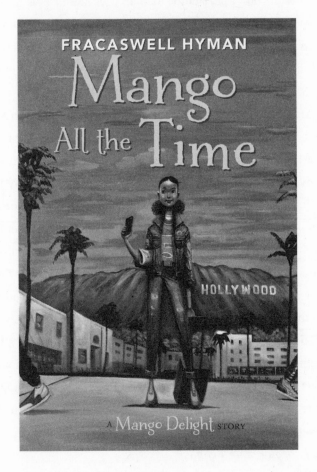

FRACASWELL HYMAN

Mango
All the Time

A Mango Delight STORY

Turn the page to start reading an excerpt from the final
book in Fracaswell Hyman's Mango Delight series!

. . .

It was before sunrise and time to head to the airport. Maxwell Paige had sent a car for us, so we said goodbye to Mom upstairs in our apartment. Jasper was sound asleep when I kissed him on his soft, peach-fuzz cheek. He had grown so much in the weeks I'd been in New York. He could even pronounce "Mango" clearly now. I have to admit, I kind of missed the way he used to say Mamo-Mamo all the time.

Heavy clouds hung ominously low in the sky, and thunder rumbled in the distance as we climbed into the town car. Not exactly ideal weather for taking off in a plane to fly across the country. I snuggled in close to Dada as we pulled away from our building. I felt a tingle, a sort of electric current running through me, as I thought about heading for a new adventure. The "tingle" was both positive and negative, because anyone who has ever read an adventure knows that there are downsides and upsides. Unexpected obstacles you have to confront and overcome . . . or not. Challenges you weren't exactly prepared for that you must conquer . . . or not. You always hope things will turn out all right. Sometimes they do, and sometimes your hopes float away like dandelion fluff. I'd had my share of roller coaster adventures over the past year. Was I ready to face more ups and downs? I sighed and thought, *Ready or not, here I come.*

When we arrived at the airport, TJ was there waiting. Maxwell Paige had sent a car for him, too, but no one accompanied him. TJ's Mohawk hair looked smooshed to one side, like he hadn't tried to do anything with it since he woke up, but his kiwi-green eyes and smile were bright. I was so happy to see him. TJ was sort of my boyfriend . . . or the closest thing to a boyfriend if I had one. I mean, if you break it down, he was a friend and a boy, but not just a regular friend. TJ was a boy who *like-liked* me and I *like-liked him* . . . but he was not an actual boyfriend.

Anywho, TJ's mother agreed to let Dada chaperone him on the flight across country, since she was busy preparing for her wedding to a man who would become TJ's stepfather. TJ didn't come right out and say it, but I had the feeling he didn't care for his mom's fiancé very much. TJ wasn't the type to talk a lot about his home life, but if you listened closely to his songs, you could tell what was really going on in his heart. He did tell me that he was looking forward to spending time with his biological father, Malachi Gatt, a corporate lawyer who lived and worked in L.A. It had been almost a year since he'd seen his dad in person.

A weird thing happened at the gate as we were about to board. When the agent called for priority and first-class passengers to begin boarding, Dada, TJ, and I walked forward and were first in line. (Maxwell Paige had the producers arrange first-class travel.) The gate agent smiled and said, "Sorry for your misunderstanding, but this call is for *first-class* and priority passengers only. Step back, and we'll call you with your group."

A red-faced man behind us carrying a garment bag sighed

and started to move around me. Dada put up his hand to the man, saying, "Hold on, please, sir." He turned to the agent and showed the tickets on his phone. TJ showed his phone too. "I believe we have seats in the first-class cabin. Group One, if I'm not mistaken."

The agent blushed, cleared her throat, and said, "Oh, of course . . . I just . . . People often make mistakes and . . . *uh* . . . welcome. Go right ahead and board." The whole thing was so weird and awkward. As we walked down the jetway to board, I asked, "What was that about?"

Dada shook his head. "Never mind. Just ignorance, that's all. Forget about it." He smiled and winked at me, but something about his eyes told me he wasn't brushing it off as easily as he asked me to.

Heavy raindrops were beating against the airplane window as we buckled our seat belts. Dada let TJ and me sit together in the two comfy leather seats in the second row of the cabin. He sat in the aisle seat directly across from us. This was a very different flight from the one I had been on earlier in the summer. The seats were way wider, and I actually had room to stretch my long legs. Dada fell asleep as soon as he sat down. TJ was quiet and kept fiddling with a guitar pick, rolling it from finger to finger.

"Wasn't it kind of embarrassing being stopped at the gate like that in front of everybody?"

"Yeah, but I think she wound up more embarrassed than we did."

"Why?"

"Because, she just assumed we didn't belong in first class because . . . well, you know."

Yeah, I guess I did know, but it wasn't something I wanted to talk about or think about. I started checking all the gadgets on the armrests. A thing to turn on the lights, a button to call the flight attendant, USB ports to charge your phone, and a little tray you could slide out to hold a cup. I couldn't help but notice TJ kept fidgeting with the guitar pick. I nudged him, "Are you nervous about the screen test?"

"No."

"About flying in the rain?"

"Uh-uh."

"Really? I am. How could you not be?"

He shrugged. "People fly in the rain all the time. Once we get above the clouds, it'll be a smooth trip. I've taken this flight before."

I gulped as the engines revved and the plane lurched forward and started picking up speed streaking down the runway. I wanted to reach for TJ's hand, but then I'd disturb his fiddling with the guitar pick, so I clenched my fists and decided to keep talking to take my mind off my nerves.

I pulled the window shade down and turned to TJ. "I'm kind of nervous about the screen test. I'm like so not a fan of tests anyway. And now, we're gonna be tested on a screen. You know, like on TV? It's gonna be like awk-weird to the max, you know? Not like doing a play where there's a separation between the audience and the cast. With TV, cameras can zoom in really close, and people can see your zits."

He looked at me. "I don't have any zits, do I?"

"No. No you don't. I'm just saying . . . you know, it's different, and I just can't understand why you're not nervous."

"Well, it's not like being on a TV sitcom is something I've always wanted. If I get on the show, cool. If not, I guess that's cool, too, but . . ." He trailed off and didn't speak for what seemed like the longest ten seconds ever, then he said, "I'm kinda hoping things go well with my dad and he wants me to move in with him though."

"You mean for good and not go back home?" This was a shocker. When we were in New York, TJ and I had confessed that we *like-liked* each other. We'd promised to hang out a lot and maybe even become girlfriend and boyfriend down the road. Now, to find out he wanted to stay in California? It felt like a tiny crack was forming in my heart. Like a fault line that could signal an earthquake.

"I'd go back home maybe for visits," he said, "but my mom is starting a new life, and I don't want to be in the way."

"Did she say you were in the way?"

"No, of course not. My mom is great. She loves me."

"What about her fiancé?"

"Mitch? I don't know. I think he wishes I weren't there.

He never says it. Not in words. But you know, I can kind of feel it when I'm around." He lifted the guitar pick to his mouth and started gnawing on it, kind of like the way I chew my fingernails when I'm nervous. "My mom doesn't want me to live with my dad though."

"Because she'd miss you?"

TJ leaned his head back and closed his eyes. "Yeah, that too. I don't really want to talk about it, Mango. We'll just see what happens."

Seems like we both had things we didn't want to talk about. I didn't want to talk about why we were stopped before boarding the plane, and TJ didn't want to talk about how his mother would feel about him moving away. I guess some things were just too tender to deal with for both of us.

I felt bad for TJ, and even though I didn't want him to move away, I hoped his father would at least *want* him to stay. Although he'd cut the conversation short, it was a good distraction from my fears. I lifted the shade and looked out the window, and TJ was right: we were high above the clouds, and the sun was shining bright, reflecting on tufts of snowy white cotton balls below us.

FRACASWELL HYMAN is an award-winning television writer, screenwriter, and actor. He is also a playwright, theater and television director, and producer who has created and executive-produced successful live-action animated television series (*The Famous Jett Jackson*, *Romeo*, and *Taina*), for Disney and Nickelodeon, earning him Peabody, Alma, and Humanitas awards. And his Netflix educational web series, *Bookmarks*, received a Kidscreen Award in 2021.

Fracaswell lives with his family in Wilmington, North Carolina, and can be found online at fracaswellhyman.com and on Instagram @fracaswell.